A LADY PIRA

# OVER RAGING TIDES

For love
and luck

JENNIFER ELLISION

*Jen Ellision*

Over Raging Tides
Jennifer Ellision
Copyright 2018 by Jennifer Ellision.

*for the girls who chart their own courses*

*From the ship's articles of the* Lady Luck:

*Any woman in want of a life at sea shall be permitted to join the ship's crew.*

# 1

My feet haven't touched dry land in one hundred and two days.

But they move assuredly along the planks of the *Lady Luck*, twisting and turning in steps that are as natural to me as breathing. I shuffle backward as Captain Ilene's cutlass bears down on mine. The sea and wind are in my ears, the clash of steel in my blood. My sword sings in my hand, and the captain's mouth is a grim line.

I have her this time.

I feint to the right, smelling victory, but Ilene's sword hooks the handle of mine as easily as if she's threaded a needle and it spills from my grasp. My hands are raised into the air, surrendering, by the time the point of her sword hovers at my throat.

"I yield, Captain."

Her smile tilts to one side as she sheathes her sword. She claps me on my back. "You nearly had me there, Gracie."

"I know." I'm smug and without a right to be. It earns me a good-natured wallop as I collect my sword from its felled spot on the deck.

It's only the night crew about us at this late hour; only the moon and stars trying valiantly to illuminate our way in the evening fog. My eyes drift up the main mast to the crow's nest, barely visible in this light. All of the night crew *should* be at the ready, but if I know Sam one bit, she's asleep up there right now. I remind myself to climb up and check after the captain retires to her cabin.

But Sam isn't the sole perpetrator. The whole crew gets lax during long stretches like this. Even *I* haven't been as rigorous with my daily tasks as I usually am.

We're far from any of the trade routes. The sea is vast and wide, and it seems like we're the only ones in it, sailing to the ends of the earth. But a royal ship could come upon us all too easily, a captain at its helm with something to prove, who thinks that a captured pirate ship would make for a lovely medal on his pretty white sash. Or we could just as easily find ourselves in the sights of another crew of buccaneers.

All that's to say, there's a time for sleeping, and it isn't while on the job. Not on any crew where *I'm* the quartermaster and first mate.

Captain Ilene collapses and pats the seat beside her. Panting, she pulls a flask from her belt and offers it to me.

"Well fought. Well fought, indeed." Her eyes are absent. The words are sincere, but her mind isn't present at the moment. At least, not until my fingers brush hers, accepting her offer of a drink. Then her stare snaps to me, sharp and assessing.

"So," she says quietly. "What news, Gracie?"

If it was gossip she was after, she'd already have it. There aren't many secrets aboard the *Luck*. In actuality, she's curious about the mood of the others. If we spend too long at sea without giving the crew a proper break, they're liable to snap, to be distracted under pressure. As quartermaster, the captain relies on me to keep an eye on the crew and gauge their mutterings before they become a problem.

I lay my sword to the side, put the flask to my lips thoughtfully as I mull over the crew's recent talk. I know she won't revel in my report

"We'll have to make for land soon," I tell her reluctantly, knowing she'll be less than pleased.

True to my predictions, she groans loudly. Her boots land with a thump on the planks as she leans forward.

I feel no joy in the news myself. I might as well be a newborn filly when we're on land, lurching about like walking is a skill that's entirely new to me. My knees knock together and wobble beneath me. It's nothing like standing on the deck of the *Luck,* riding the movement of the ocean.

"The crew's restless," I tell her. "They need a few nights in a tavern, chance to walk around a town, use their coin for something they may not precisely *need,* but can take pleasure in. Besides that, we're low on supplies and unless you want a ship crewed by women crippled with scurvy, then—"

Laughing, she holds up a hand for me to stop as her white sleeves ripple in the breeze. "Grace. I wasn't arguing, if you'll recall."

My shoulders relax. "No. You weren't. Sorry, Captain."

She lets loose a loud groan, stretching her arms into the air. "We'll plot a course for Cielito in the morn. See if you can get us a proper heading tonight." Her hand lands on my shoulder. "And get some rest, Gracie."

"You too, Captain."

She nods and walks off into the distance, heading for her bunk and quarters.

Me? I'll sleep eventually. But right now my mind is buzzing from the energy of our duel, and the air is heavy. It feels like something is waiting out there, beneath the dark waters and reflection of the moon's orb. But there's naught that I can do about it. Whatever it is will wait until it's good and ready to make itself known. As much as I'd like to, it's not as though I can dive into the waters' depths and face it head-on.

At least...I couldn't and live to tell the tale.

Belatedly, I realize that my sword still hangs heavy in my hand, and I return it to its sheath once more. If I'm not going to be able to sleep, I might as well check on the night crew. Sam, in particular.

I make my way across the top deck and hover beneath the crow's nest, listening for the telltale sounds of Sam's snores. But all's quiet above me. Not even a stray breeze flapping the sails.

"I'm awake, Miss Porter." Sam's voice drifts down to my ears, tired and wry.

I grin. She caught me.

"One can never be sure, Miss Smi." I call back good-naturedly before loping away to look over the ship's rails. Any crew woman walking by will think that I'm escaping the stale air of my cabin, searching for a salty breeze to caress my face. They won't notice the tense set of my shoulders or the hard light in my eyes as they scan the sea's surface for the danger that waits below.

I can't go into the sea to fight the Mordgris myself. But I can certainly be on my guard for them.

Because, at sunset, I'd seen the first sign of trouble that had come in days: a flash of gray chasing our bow. I'd been on the lookout ever since.

But if Sam—our *actual* lookout—hadn't seen it, maybe I'd imagined it. I *wished* I'd imagined it. I said nothing of it to the captain, to Celia, not even to Sam. Maybe, for a moment, I managed to convince myself that it was a fin. A fish or perhaps a shark—even some sort creature that lives below the surface and benevolently allows us to skim the sea above.

I'm not sure I believed that. Not even for a brief, fleeting moment. After all, the Mordgris and I have met before.

Now, though, there's only the weak light of the moon skimming the waves below the fog, so I stifle a yawn against the back of my hand.

To sleep, then.

After all, if it *was* the Mordgris I'd seen…they'd let me know it soon enough.

But despite these peaceful intentions, the distant crash of a cannon smashes through the quiet. I whip my head around, barely registering the slap of my braid on my cheek as I search for the boom's source.

And I know instantly that it was stupid to believe that the silver tail I'd seen could have been a shark when the Mordgris have haunted me for years.

That flash of them in the waves below... I should have known this night would bring trouble.

The response is instantaneous as the ship comes alive around me. Captain Ilene bursts from her quarters, yanking a boot on.

"*Grace?*" The bellow reaches me as I stand halfway across the ship by the swing guns. It's a demand for information, for a report. It's a, *Godsdammit, why didn't you wake me if we were being fired upon?*

"Not ours, Captain," I call, squinting into the night. "The *Luck's* not even nicked."

Lila, our master gunner, settles into her spot at the guns, giving me a curt nod in greeting. The crew ceases its scramble around me, and Sam stands at my elbow. The straw hat she usually wears to protect her face is missing, probably left behind in the crow's nest, and her freckles are stark against her cheeks.

"Nice of you to warn us of another crew about, lookout," I mutter.

"I rightly predicted that they'd have the decency to announce their entrance," she retorts.

"How did you fall asleep so fast? We spoke not five minutes ago."

She shrugs. "It's a gift. Besides..." She motions to the haze that surrounds us. "Much good would it have done if I'd been awake. I have excellent eyes, but even I can't see a damn thing."

"Because they weren't firing at us." The captain appears next to me, blown there like vapor. She lowers the spyglass from her eye. "It's warships we've stumbled on."

A respectful hush falls over those of us who've heard her. We've steered clear of the war thus far. We all hail from different lands, but that matters not. Our loyalties are not to any queen or king. We're for ship, for sea, for crew. And most importantly, for ourselves.

Still, it was only a matter of time until we sashayed our way between those fighting for kings and queens who wouldn't even notice their deaths.

Word reached us on our last stop for supplies that things between Tigri and Allaria had come to a head, but it's a different world out here on the sea. Sometimes, it feels like it's just us and the Mordgris left.

An illusion that is clearly meant to disappear now.

The captain stows the spyglass in her belt. "Miss Smi?" Sam inclines her head toward the captain, her ear tilted in a fashion that makes it clear that she's listening. "Kindly see yourself back to your post."

Sam salutes, yawning, and lopes away, ambling up to the crow's nest like a loose-limbed primate, swinging for the trees it calls home.

I watch her go, watch the captain's jaw clench minutely at her laissez-faire attitude. Sam's movements may have been slow, her manner nonchalant, but the captain missed what I saw. She didn't see the alert look in Sam's eyes. Fog or not, she's going to stare out at the sea and stare *hard,* unwilling to miss anything else as she scolds herself for failing to spot the other ship.

"Captain...?" I venture the tentative prod, and Captain Ilene looks to me.

Her teeth are a quick flash of white in my direction. "Worry not, Gracie. We're just going to have ourselves a little look-see."

Now that I'm aware the ships are there, I can just make out their shapes in the distance, shadows on the horizon, darker spots of gray amidst all of the vaporous fog. The pelt of gunfire comes quickly now, little *pop-pop-pops* in the distance, each sounding just a bit farther than the other, likely fired from different pistols.

Captain Ilene takes the helm from Celia's capable hands and eases the *Luck* through the sea, drifting closer to the battle, near enough to see the indistinct ships just a bit clearer. The shots are slower now; there are fewer people left alive to fire them.

One ship melts into the ocean, frighteningly clear of the movement that would indicate life on-board. On the other, there are blurs of movement—arms raised in victory, a manning of their stations.

We sit. Shrouded in fog, in the quiet, we're buoyed by the gentle tide. Soon, the only sounds are the quiet lap of the waves against our ship's sides and the anticipatory breathing of the crew around me. Like lions, waiting to pounce upon a meal, only awaiting a signal from the dominant one among us. The surviving warship leaves after a time, pushing through the wreckage of their felled foe. I don't know if they see us, if they even bother to look around before they determine their heading and sail off in another direction, but when they're gone, we start toward the leftovers of their opponent.

We're searching for a bounty. Anything that survived long enough to float that we can sell off. Coins are too much to hope for; they sink so quickly it's almost like they dive down to the bottom of the depths. But there are other things we may yet scrounge. A chest of paper notes would be buoyant. Or a gold masthead still attached to a plank may be enough to keep it above the surface.

I catch a flash of silver undulating alongside the *Luck* and swallow hard. *Mordgris.* Is it the ship they're after? Or me?

"Captain." It's a rasp at first, and I have to try again, repeating her name until she cocks an acknowledging eyebrow in my direction. "I'm not certain this is worth our time," I say once I have her attention.

I don't want to tell her it's the Mordgris. That they've followed me...again. At a certain point, one has to ask themselves when their risk finally begins to outweigh their reward.

But if we keep moving toward the ship, it's not a secret I'll be able to keep. Captain Ilene will notice them soon enough.

Even aside from the Mordgris, I'd hate this. I *hate* collecting treasure like this. It's not earned. It's like we're scavengers, vultures preying on a carcass.

"Dear gods."

I think it's my voice that utters the oath when we finally get to the carnage. What is left is charred, somehow still smoking even as it sinks into the water's depths. Our ship thumbs aside limp bodies still pink with the rapidly fading glow of life.

"Select your crew, Gracie." The captain murmurs at my side and squeezes my shoulder before gathering her own women.

I take a small group in a longboat, choosing to row instead of hoisting the sails all of our longboats possess; the better to comb carefully through the waves. We descend the *Luck*'s side slowly. Gods, there are *so* many bodies here. Men of all ages, wet hair limp over their eyes, the stain of gunpowder and smoke left behind. Some have already sunk to the ocean below, weighed down by the heavy uniforms and medals that they wear.

My eyes flick over a tiny movement—so minor that I nearly miss it. But when I focus on the motion, my breath catches. A dark head lifts, wary, but hopeful. It's too far to see any great detail, but his eyes glint, shining in the light of his fiery ship. I swear his eyes stay locked on mine as we stare at each other across the dark sea. He doesn't stir. Doesn't call out for help. It's as though he's waiting to see what we'll do first.

There is a smaller figure beside him, the bigger one's arm wrapped protectively around him as they float on something—a door? I'm not sure.

*Survivors.* My heart stutters in my chest. Somehow, *impossibly*, they'd made it out of the doomed wreck.

But their safety is not yet assured. In my peripheral vision, I suddenly see a silver shadow behind me streak toward them, and I dive, moving before I'm conscious of doing so. I won't let the Mordgris take another. Not today. I cut powerful strokes through the waves, kicking feet weighed down with boots.

"Leave him!" The captain's voice is a hoarse shriek echoing over the waters. The crew on her longboat release startled grunts as she darts to the side of the longboat. "*Grace!* I said, *leave him.*"

My jaw hardens. I won't.

I'm closer to the door and the boys, and that counts for something. Despite the Mordgris's speed, I make it there first.

"Help me up," I demand. Wordlessly, the older boy complies, dark eyes wide, and I scrabble back on my hindquarters, tugging at my belt, just in time.

My pistol wavers as I level it at the Mordgris's head. The threat is meaningless. The gunpowder is wet, rendering the gun useless, but I chance that the Mordgris know only that these objects kill. That they'd work just as well to blow away their gods-be-damned heads as mortal ones.

I swallow hard, never having been this close to one before. It's wholly unsettling to feel seen and held in a gaze when a creature's eyes are consumed by the pitch black of a night sky. The Mordgris has gray skin, stretched tight over cartilage where a nose should be. Its teeth are rows upon rows of needles as it hisses at me, backing away, webbed claws raised as it sinks into the water. My hands are shaking, but I don't dare lower my weapon until I can no longer see its silver sheen beneath the water. Only then do I holster it.

"Thank you," comes the voice behind me, and I start. Locked in a silent battle of wills with the Mordgris— who would attack or withdraw first?—I had nearly forgotten the boys that had spurred me to action in the first place.

"Don't thank me yet," I reply grimly. Captain Ilene's crew rows toward us, her eyes murderous.

We have plenty of rules on the *Lady Luck*. But chief among them is this:

We don't take men on-board.

*From the ship's articles of the* Lady Luck:

*No man shall board this ship.*

I'm sopping wet when they haul me back aboard the longboat, braid dripping wetly onto my toes. The captain's crew bobs a good distance away. Her gaze burns into me, but I pointedly avoid looking in her direction.

Instead, I turn my eyes onto the wet, huddled, terrified masses still floating on the door that the warship left behind. The older boy's expression has twisted into a scowl, pushing the younger one—his brother?—behind him protectively. The little one's eyes are huge in his face as he peers out from behind his brother's knee.

By now, I think the older boy has worked out what we are. There isn't a uniform among us. Just weapons and dirt, boats and breasts.

I turn from them. If they want their lives saved, they'll put aside any moral quibbles they have with the ideas of piracy or women sailing the Eleven Seas.

"Pull the lads on-board," I command my small crew, unknotting my braid and wringing the water from it.

"The captain won't like it," someone offers.

I plop down onto the longboat's bench, occupying myself with inspecting my boots. Damn. As if the smells aboard the *Luck* aren't bad enough. These will stink to high heavens for weeks to come.

"The captain's not in charge of this longboat, is she?" Grunts come as I remove a boot and pour the water over the side. Back into the ocean from whence it came. "She put *me* in charge of it, didn't she?"

At this, the girls grumble, but they know the argument makes sense. We all voted on the captain, on the ship's articles. And the rules are simple. You do what the captain says. And *she* said to follow me.

The crew stretch their dirty hands into the water to haul the boys, who hesitantly accept their offer, up. Once on-board, they eye each other distrustfully. The little one scoots himself into a corner beside old Molly, who offers him a wide smile and pats the bench beside her.

He cringes away from her blackened and missing teeth, back into the comforting wing of protection his brother offers him.

By now, the sky is lightening. Dawn is near. I sigh. "Back to the *Luck*," I command.

"But we've not found a single thing to take back!" one of the girls protests.

"Look around!" I snap. "I see mere splinters of wood left. Do you fancy hours out here combing through that for nothing?"

"The captain won't—"

"She won't like it. I know." I massage my temples. "You." I point at the boys.

The older one raises a single dark brow over murky brown eyes. "Yes?"

"It's a warship, yeah?"

He stiffens. "It *was.* If you're with those Tigrid rebels--"

"You have eyes in your head, and unless you're missing a brain up there, you know what we are. I could care less about the war, boy. We don't answer to a crown. I'm more concerned with whether or not there was a treasure to be had on-board."

His eyes widen. "Treasure?"

Unmistakably, his eyes flicker down to his small companion, who shakes his head violently. They're definitely brothers; I'm certain of it now. They have the same stubborn set to their mouths, the same green clouding their brown eyes. The younger one looks more than a little worn, but he stands upright with the bigger boy's hand firm on his shoulder.

"We worked in the galley, miss," the older one says smoothly. "It wasn't for us to know if there was a treasure to be had."

My left foot, they worked in the galley. Even as soaked as they are, the quality of their clothing and their cultured accents set them apart from the rest of the rabble.

He knows if there was treasure on-board. I'm sure of it. But I shrug off the instinct. Treasure or not, there will be others, and I want to get free of this wreck, where I'm certain the Mordgris are lurking in the shadows waiting for another chance to strike.

"Back to the *Luck*," I order again, more emphatically. This time, the girls hoist their oars in hand and heave us toward the *Lady Luck*, waiting in the distance. It is a hulking shadow, dark and gray. Intimidating to those who don't know her. But it's home.

When we reach her familiar sails, the rest of the crew hauls us back on-board. We're already hoisted in the air, dangling at the *Luck's* side when the captain's longboat and a third, also deployed to search for treasure, make it back. I'm glad. The fact that we've returned first gives me a few more precious moments free from her wrath.

Some of the girls recoil when we're hauled on-board— owing, no doubt, to the unexpected invasion of males. We all have different stories, different degrees of liking toward them. Personally, I just never found men that useful. They'd certainly never done anything for me.

Some of the others are pleased. We may not have come bearing jewels, but we sure found *something.*

"Miss Porter," Celia purrs. The captain left her in charge of the *Luck* while we were out scavenging. She saunters up to us, flicking her saber from its sheath to run its tip over the older one's boot. "It seems that you found a treasure after all."

I kick the sword away mulishly, and she pouts. "Spoilsport."

"Get our guests some refreshments," I call loudly.

"Gracie," old Maude tries, knotting her hands in her apron. "The captain won't—"

I continue to pull rank. "Unless you've all been struck dumb by blows on the head, I expect no one has forgotten that I am, in fact, still the quartermaster on-board the *Lady Luck?* That the captain is not here and thus rank falls to me?"

I place a cocky hand on my hip, jut it out to one side. My hand lingers on the hilt of my pistol, at the empty sheath where my sword usually rests. I know no one misses the implicit threat. Captain Ilene is the only person who still beats me in a match.

"Someone get our guests some refreshments." I have a hope of having the boys already in the galley when Ilene arrives, so I can explain my lapse in judgement. Men aren't my favorite breed, but even a decision made in haste is a decision made and I'll be damned if I'm not going to stand by it.

Celia's lifts a lazy hand into the air. "I suppose I could volunteer, Miss Porter."

Well, of course she does. Sighing, I nod, giving her permission to proceed.

Sam scrambles down from the crow's nest and lurches to a stop beside me. "Heads up. Captain, ahoy." She barely moves her mouth with the muttered aside.

There's no need for me to respond. The whole crew knows that the captain won't be pleased with me. I've broken our cardinal rule. I've allowed a man—*men,* that should be plural; even worse—on-board the *Luck,* and it won't be allowed to go unremarked upon.

The captain's longboat hasn't even stopped swinging before she's heaved herself over the side and onto the deck. She strides through the crowd and seizes me by the ear without a word. I have to work to keep pace with her, lest my ear be parted from my head.

"My quarters," she snaps—needlessly, as though I hadn't already worked out where we were off to. "*Now.*"

Captain Ilene's quarters are the finest on the ship, as they should be. It wouldn't do for a captain to have anything less than that what befits her station. An oak table is bolted to the floor, and it stretches the length of her sitting room.

Her steps, heavy and clunky as she paces in the small space, echo around us, but I don't fill the pulses of silence between them, waiting for her to speak first. Finally, she flings herself into one of the chairs, apparently spent.

"You want to explain yourself to me?" she asks, massaging her temple with eyes closed, a habit I picked up from her.

"Explaining..." I hedge, enunciating the word like it's a foreign thing I've never had the chance to taste before. "Ah, that's... Well, it's not the *highest* of things on my wish list at the moment, Captain," I manage.

She simply glares.

I see. Not the time for quips and witticisms then.

I cast about for an explanation that does not involve the Mordgris, hesitant to introduce them into this moment, like one more mark against me. Sadly, I draw a blank, coming up with nothing.

My shoulders lift in a shrug, giving up on an alternative explanation. "It was *them,* ma'am," I say helplessly.

Her brows, furrowed, now clear as she straightens in her seat. "*Them?* You mean the Mordgris. Again?"

I nod unhappily.

She sighs. "They do dog your steps, don't they, Gracie?"

"Yes, ma'am."

"But the boys…"

"If it was something the Mordgris wanted, it was something I didn't want them to have. I'm not sorry," I say fiercely, meaning it as I clench my fists.

"You never are." The words are quiet as she eyes me speculatively from beneath the brim of her black hat. She rolls an apple back and forth across the table between her hands. "Tell me true now: is this about your mother?"

"*No.*" I deny it vehemently, banishing the mention of my mother back into the ether where it belongs, and I force myself to say what I know she wants to hear: "Mama's dead, Captain."

Despite expecting it—despite *wanting* me to remind us both—her eyes shutter and her breath quickens with the reiteration as I go on. "This is just about me. Me and the Mordgris."

She regains her composure with a few calming breaths and considers me. "They can't stay," she says, testing my acceptance of these terms.

I find them quite amenable and nod, tension leaving me. "I'm aware."

At my acquiescence, she deflates and sinks into a chair. "Don't think I'll be letting you make a habit of this, Gracie— saving every wayward man we come across. It would just be two less cocks out there to screw us over. But as we're heading to port at Cielito anyway…" She sighs. "Fine. We'll take them that far. I'll let you have this one. But you'll be swabbing the deck tonight."

This is more than a fair penance for defying orders and ignoring our charter. I nod.

Like a petulant child, she pouts her lips. "I *do* wish that we were going back in with some treasure to our names, though."

"Actually…" a rough voice breaks in. I turn to the doorway to see the older boy that I'd rescued now fully upright and standing in Captain Ilene's doorway.

His lips quirk up. "We may be able to help with that."

*From the ship's articles of the* Lady Luck:

*The captain and quartermaster shall each be awarded private chambers.*

3

Captain Ilene's mouth slams into a hard line at the interruption, and the lazy nonchalance with which the boy has dared to insert himself into ship matters vanishes as he swallows hard at the look in her eyes.

"Have you a name, young man?"

This "man" is no older than I am. But he's soft. You can tell it from the look in his eyes. Never had to fight for more than what's been given to him. It's always been enough.

He won't find any compatriots in that manner on-board the *Luck*. We're all different enough, but one thing is for certain: none of us have ever been given what we deem enough. It's the constant battle for *more* that led us to where we are.

"I'm Leo, ma'am."

At least he has the sense to offer some deference.

"No surname that goes with that?" she prods.

"Wesson," he hastily offers. "And the little one's Wesson, too. My brother, John."

"Mr. Wesson, then," Ilene says. "Were you not left in the care of my very able crew?"

"Yes, ma'am. But I—"

"So instead of accepting our very *generous* hospitality, you took it upon yourself to sneak away. Sly, Mr. Wesson. Very sly. A fox in a proverbial henhouse—though perhaps that is a bit on-the-nose. But let's continue on with this metaphor, regardless. Foxes are a *nuisance,* Mr. Wesson. And when a farmer grows tired of a pest disrupting the hen's business, what do you supposed that farmer may do?"

Wesson stays silent, though the anger he's not well-trained enough to hide lights his eyes. He's no imbecile. He perceives the threat that Captain Ilene is offering with all the lightness of polite dinner conversation.

"The farmer may choose to *exterminate* that pest, Mr. Wesson."

Now the anger truly flares in his eyes. "The farmer may have to catch the fox first," he says quietly.

*Interesting.* My estimation of him rises minutely.

The captain's brow raises, and she nods to me. While she reclines in her seat and lazily rests her feet upon her table, I cross the room and, with little effort, toe the door to the captain's quarters closed. A scant second later and the bolt is flipped.

The captain motions to Wesson as if passing him the bread at dinner, her lips quirked slightly in amusement. The implication is clear:

The fox has been caught. And the farmer didn't even have to lift a finger to catch him.

Wesson nods, taking her point. "It's your henhouse, ma'am. I'm happy to take my treasure to the next farm."

"Oh, for the love of—" I release an annoyed huff of air. "You're both very clever, congratulations. Captain?" I turn to her and quirk an eyebrow. "By your leave, may we dispense with this metaphor and speak plainly?"

"As you wish, Miss Porter."

"Thank you." I turn back to the man in our midst. "Mr. Wesson, you claimed not to know of any treasure. What's changed?"

He hesitates. "John thought it best not to tell when we weren't certain which crown you were loyal to."

"We are loyal only to ourselves," I inform him.

"And that, madam, is precisely why I have chosen to unburden myself to you. So long as you are not working with an enemy of my king, I can be no worse off than I am now."

I lean toward him, tilting my head. "What is to stop us from simply relieving you and your brother of this treasure? You'd present little challenge to us."

"A crew of *women?*" He snorts. "Please. Have you a strongman on-board?"

I stiffen in fury, and the captain's boots thunk down onto the floor.

"It is a fool who underestimates a woman because of her sex, Mr. Wesson," I say, hearing a slight tremble in my voice that betrays my rage. "And an ungrateful one who forgets who just saved his life."

He has the decency to look contrite, though that disintegrates into barely veiled rage as I continue.

"Your brother is being fed in our mess as we speak. What is to stop us from tipping a vial of poison into his food?"

His eyes narrow. "I would hope that a sense of honor—"

I bark out a laugh. "If it was not abundantly clear, Mr. Wesson, you have found yourself aboard a *pirate* ship. Female pirates, yes, but pirates nonetheless. There are many things in our code, but honor is not one of them."

He has no clever retort for that.

"*As I was saying.* It is a fool who discounts our abilities. You look able-bodied, Mr. Wesson, but I somehow doubt you've trained with a sword. Perhaps you prefer a pistol. Ah, but you're unarmed as well."

"*If* I had one," he says with a sort of lethal quiet that would put fear into a lesser woman, "you'd see that I am an excellent shot."

My lips curve with the challenge, eyes locked with his. "But you don't."

I'm impatient with this talk now and cross to the door, wanting only to escape this imbecile. I should have left him to the Mordgris. "There are many dead fools who have underestimated me, Mr. Wesson. Do you intend to join their ranks?"

His mouth opens, a retort hot on his tongue, but he bites it back, grinding his teeth. "No."

"No...?" I prod, arms crossed and an expectant brow raised.

"No, *ma'am*." He spits the word out like it's burned him.

"Very good, Mr. Wesson. Let me see your hands," I order.

Looking surprised, Wesson nonetheless obeys, extending them palms down.

I take each of them in my mine, turning them over. Internally I marvel at their softness. I don't think I've ever touched skin so soft. I run a finger along his right hand, where fingers meet palm. It's smooth. On my own hands, that spot is marred with healed-over blisters, rough calluses. I have a sailor's hands.

"Lovely," I compliment him, voice low. "Very soft. Indeed, these are some well-taken-care-of hands."

"Thank you?" he answers, a question in his voice.

"You haven't worked a day in your life, have you?"

He stiffens, taking offense. "I grew up the son of Lord Lukas Wesson."

Ugh. A nobleman. The worst of the worst.

"My work has typically been limited to leisure and scholarly pursuits. But..." I'd have to be deaf, dumb, and blind to ignore the feel of his stare, the way the tone of his voice grows gravelly as he adds, "...that doesn't mean I can't be *useful*."

The implication in his voice leads me to believe he has more use for himself in mind than just tying knots and swabbing the deck.

I jerk my head up, meet his smirking brown eyes, and throw his hand away as though it's a slug I've found hiding in my stew.

"You entered my chambers offering assistance procuring treasure, Mr. Wesson. How is it that you propose to help us?" Captain Ilene prompts, reminding us both why Wesson's intrusion into her cabin is still permitted. "I'd have to agree with my quartermaster here that you don't appear naturally inclined to life on-board a ship."

"Quite right, back to it." He clears his throat and straightens up. "I presume you've heard of the Map of Omna?"

I roll my eyes and scoff. Of course we've heard of the Map of Omna. *Everyone's* heard of it. Named for the famed goddess of wisdom, the patron of discovery, it's a magical map, spelled to be all but omniscient. It knows the precise location of every treasure. You have only to ask where you might find something to see the route scrawl itself across the paper.

As nice as it would be to believe such a thing exists, it's the stuff of fairytales. Of mysticism. Of legend.

"The map is a myth," the captain says with great certainty. "I know that better than most."

She does, too. The only reason I wound up on Captain Ilene's ship is because of her quest for the map. In her younger years, she'd followed every rumor, every *whisper* of its location. She'd been on-board enemy ships in disguise, combed through deserted islands, and come up with nothing.

It can find anything. Treasure, legends, people thought lost… there isn't anything that can hide from it. It can unearth anything you wish. If *I* had it in my possession, I know exactly who—and what—I'd look for.

"It's not a myth," he shoots back, just as certain. "I've seen it. I've *held* it in my—" he spares a scant glance in my direction "—'well-taken-care-of' hands."

Wesson explains his story. He and his brother, John, were aboard the *Assurance*, an Allarian royal navy vessel. To hear him tell it, it wasn't war they were off to. No, they were on a mission. A mission, he tells us, with earnest eyes, delivered to them by the Allarian king himself.

They were to retrieve the map and see it safely back to king and country. Their ship was filled to the brim with scholars and explorers, people who were well-suited to the task of finding an ancient, mysterious map, if it so existed.

And exist, it did.

But there was the rub. Scholars, explorers, and noblemen aren't much help when it comes to defending a ship. When they were set upon by a Tigrid ship, they could barely muster up the *suggestion* of a defense.

The Tigrids boarded their ship, finding the map with ease.

"Our ship was filled with honorable men. There wasn't," he says, looking away, his voice growing quiet, "a great deal of secrecy over its location on-board. And they revealed it quickly in an attempt to save their lives. Didn't matter, as the Tigrid rebels slit their throats anyway."

So he'd been sailing amongst cowards and idiots, not even quick enough on their feet to think of a convincing lie.

"How did the two of you manage to survive?" I wonder.

"We were lucky," he says simply. Matter-of-fact. "When they boarded the ship, John and I were at the opposite end. I held my hand over his mouth so that he'd be quiet and they wouldn't find us. And I waited for an opportunity. I got us into a longboat and had nearly managed to lower it to the water when a cannon struck the *Assurance* and threw us overboard. The ship caught flame, I found a piece of the wreck big enough to hold us both, and we watched as it and everyone we knew on-board sank into the waves."

"And that is where we stand today," Wesson says. "The map is in the hands of dishonorable enemies, and *we* are in the hands of dishonorable—"

I raise a brow.

"We are in the hands of...pirates," he finished lamely.

"Why did he send you after the map in the first place? Is he a great seeker of treasure, this king of yours?" I ask nonchalantly, trying not to betray the way my pulse is quickening in my throat. I fight not to exchange a glance with Ilene, knowing how badly we both want this. Gods above, if he speaks true and we could find the map... We'd be rich. We'd be *invincible,* able to rule the Eleven Seas. Pirate queens, the lot of us. That would show all the men who thought women on-board a ship would bring nothing but bad luck.

"The Map of Omna doesn't work only as a means to unearth treasure, Miss...?" He trails off, waiting for me to fill in the silence.

"Gracie here is the ship's quartermaster," the Captain says.

"Miss will do fine," I say loudly. *'Gracie,' Captain?*

*Honestly…* "Or Quartermaster Porter, if you prefer."

"Lord Leonardo Wesson," he says with a mocking imitation of a bow. "If *you* prefer."

"I do not."

The captain is unsuccessful in reining in a chuckle.

"What I *do* prefer, Mr. Wesson, is talk of treasure."

"As I was saying, Miss Porter. The map—like myself—has many uses. My king is trying to win a war. Imagine, being able to find the precise location of people to capture, of enemy ships that would attack us. *Imagine* being able to find and disable them before they could work against us!" Almost, it seems, without his knowledge, his hands clench themselves into fists. "I just can't fathom it in the hands of those Tigrid rebels."

He straightens. "I offer you a bargain, Captain. Help me retrieve the Map of Omna. Once found, we'll use it to locate any treasure you like before I return it to my king."

"What's to stop us from simply using you to get it and seeing you right over the side of the ship?

He looks smug, and I twitch. I'd like to smack that expression right off his spoiled little face. "There are things I know about the map that no one left alive has discovered. I'd wager none of your crew has much in the way of formal education. The map doesn't offer its wisdom in the common tongue. It's magicked in the Word of the Ancient Ones."

The Word of the Ancient Ones is an all but dead language. In days long since passed, it was used in religious services and was taught only to the upper echelons of society. These days, it's mostly only religious scholars and idle nobles who bother to learn it.

And young, female pirates who need a new language to add to their studies.

The Word of the Ancient Ones *also* happens to be one of the four languages that I speak.

Wesson has it right, in a sense. I doubt that my education was formal in the way that he means. I was never smartly dressed and was just as likely to be taken to task over an improper grip on my sword as I was for doing my sums incorrectly. But my mother and Captain Ilene had seen to it that I had a very thorough education. On land, I'd have been banished to the realms of music, sewing, and "polite" society. On the *Luck*, acquiring female tutors in exchange for safe passage and books in every port, my education has been better than even most noble*men* could hope for.

Almost imperceptibly, the captain's eyes flit to mine.

"What do you think, Miss Porter?"

"The Map of Omna, Captain," I say in a properly awed voice. "I think if we found it, there's not a soul on-board who'd regret the time spent chasing it." I fight to keep the mirth from my voice when I say, "Even if we *do* need to keep Mr. Wesson on-board for his information and translating abilities."

"I concur," she says, nodding. "It appears you have us neatly over a barrel, Mr. Wesson. You've got yourself an accord. We shall redirect to Cielito for information and be off on our quest together."

His shoulders relax infinitesimally. I hadn't realized until that moment how corded through they were with tension.

"Come with me, Mr. Wesson," I say. "If the captain gives her leave, you may follow me to the mess. We'll speak about this treasure you purport to know of at a later time. Captain?" Captain Ilene gives me a nod of permission, and Wesson clenches his fists, but moves in line behind me, ready to follow. I can feel the heat of his ire like a banked fire at my back. The threat of poisoning his younger brother has likely unnerved him, no matter how he hides it.

I unbolt the door and pause, glancing back at him. "Oh, and Mr. Wesson? Should you forget: you may be larger—perhaps even physically stronger—than many of us alone. But it is also a fool who forgets the old adage."

"There are quite a few old adages, ma'am. To which are you referring?"

I sweep my arm forward, inviting him to exit Ilene's chambers. "The one that reminds us of the strength found in numbers."

As I leave, my eyes drift back to the captain. Hers glint in the telltale shine of victory, and I let a little smile curve the corner of my lip in reply as the door swings closed behind me.

The small Wesson—John—is alive and well in the mess hall when his sullen older brother and I arrive. It's quiet among the tables—the crew ate hours ago, well before all of the excitement this evening, and those who aren't on night duty have already retired to their bunks. Little John is eagerly spooning the last of his ration of beans into his mouth, while Celia and Anne sit beside him, an amused look on Celia's face.

"Miss Porter." Celia tilts her hat in greeting.

"Miss Munn," I return.

Wesson squeezes onto the bench beside his brother, ruffling his hair in a manner that he's trying to make seem playful. But he's betrayed by the slight shaking of his hands and the flicking of his eyes to John's plate.

"Get off, Leo," John mumbles. He shrugs off his brother's touch, and Wesson rolls his eyes, satisfied that my threats were a lie.

This time, at least.

"Little whelp didn't even save me a morsel," he mutters.

"Our hospitality knows no bounds," I say dryly. "I'll see about getting you a ration. They should stretch a bit as we're making for land."

Celia's blue-gold eyes snap to mine. "Are we, now?"

"We are. Captain's giving the orders at sunrise."

A slow smile curves across her mouth. "Cielito?"

"Cielito," I confirm.

She barks out a laugh and leaps up from the bench. "Fantastic."

"I know." And then, because I can't resist taunting the prim and proper noble we've brought aboard, I add, "I haven't had a lay in ages."

Wesson's eyes shoot wide, and they dart to me.

Celia doesn't miss it. "Care to beat the island to the punch?" she asks, raising an eyebrow and jerking her chin in my direction.

Mute, he simply shakes his head.

She gives a rueful shake of her own head. "Too much woman aboard this ship for you? What a shame." She stretches, and the move elongates her form into something long and lean, reminiscent of a predatory cat, before she saunters away in the direction of the messaging seagulls. Anne trails behind her, shooting dark looks Wesson's way.

"Celia!" I call.

She turns, brow raised in question.

"Not a word about our destination until the captain

gives the order."

She gives me a mocking salute and exits the mess. I frown after her, uncertain whether or not she took me seriously. I just never know with Celia. And she hadn't changed course away from the seagulls that we use to send missives back to land or other ships.

Wesson stares open-mouthed after her for a moment before shaking his head and redirecting his attention back onto me.

"I don't guess that ladies talk that way where you're from?" I ask.

"*No one* talks that way where I'm from," he says.

"Shame. Our brand of honesty can be...refreshing." I clap him on the shoulder. "I'll go and see about those rations."

One of the benefits of securing the position of quartermaster and first mate on a ship as large as the *Luck*: there are two private cabins on-board; one for the captain and one for me. It's there that I head back to once I get the elder Wesson his rations and both of them a spot to sleep. My quarters are nothing as large as Ilene's, but it's my own little space. If I were so inclined to take a lover, I wouldn't have to settle, as the rest of the crew does, for quiet, hushed breaths and hurried fingers pressed between bodies. I wouldn't have to sacrifice privacy. I'd be able to take my time.

We each get our own ration of rum, water, and—if the journey is a long one—grog. But sometimes I need a little something extra. And my quarters is where I keep that. My hand plunges into my pocket on the walk there, seeking the rough edges of my mother's broken compass. It's useless, of course, but the memento is one of the few things I have left of her. It brings me a small measure of comfort to have it with me.

I huff out a short breath when I enter my room, finally feeling the stressful effects of the evening. Tugging the ribbon loose from my braid, I open the chest bolted to the foot of my tiny bunk to find the silver flask contained within.

After a swift sip, I close my eyes, letting it burn its way down to my belly and savoring the sensation. These are expensive sips, paid for in premium when on Cielito and the other islands. And I save each drop of the liquid for nights like these.

Because the Mordgris don't just dog my steps, as the captain said. They *haunt* me. When I close my eyes, all I see are their rows of needle teeth, laughing at me, black eyes endless empty pools. Hands that end in talons gripping my mother's flesh, pulling her from a longboat into the depths below.

I lied when the captain asked. Of course this is about my mother. It's *always* about my mother. Because without a body to prove it, I can't simply accept that she's gone. Because if she *is* gone, someone must pay for it.

And for just an instant, when I catch a glimpse of the looking glass on my way to my bunk, it's not my face that I see.

It's hers.

*From the ship's articles of the* Lady Luck*:*

*None shall relieve herself upon the deck. She who does shall be subject to five lashings upon her back.*

Our sails shift for Cielito. In between calculating the supplies we'll need for our journey and conferring with our sailing master over our course, I observe the crew from my position at the helm. Captain Ilene ties a message to a gull's foot and watches it fly off, hands on her hips. Celia sends her own message, then roughhouses with Anne, Maude, and Bonnie on deck, shoving at them and laughing. And the Wesson boys...well...

In the days following their unexpected arrival onto our ship, the boys have been put to work. The elder Leo is assigned everyone's least favorite task: swabbing the deck.

He's bent himself nearly in twain on the main deck as he shoves at the mop, determinedly putting his back into the task at hand.

In this relentless heat, relieved only by sea's gift of a sailing breeze, Wesson has also made the mistake of removing his shirt, exposing his unvarnished skin to the sun's unforgiving gaze. He'll pay for that later, I think, my eyes skimming his form. Lord Leonardo Wesson may not have much of a history of manual labor, but laziness running through his bones is clearly not to blame for that. Nor, it's clear, is gluttony a sin of his. His torso is lean, and while the muscles there are certainly not toned—not *yet*, at any rate—they peek out with every push of the mop, as though to wave hello and remind me of their owner's potential.

"Only going to make himself more sore that way," Sam says, following my eyes when I trail off.

"Do you mean the backache he's heading for from the way he's swabbing the deck or the burn he's liable to get from the sun?"

"Yes."

I snort, amused, and turning away. "He'll learn soon enough. Besides, my mother always said, mistakes are far better teachers than rules."

"That's true enough," Sam says. She pushes up the brim of her hat, swipes some sweat away, and settles it back onto her brow. It casts the freckles across her cheeks and nose into shadow. "He still trying to see the Captain?"

"Oh, yes. Our Mr. Wesson is nothing if not determined," I say. "Depending upon his mood, he either *demands* to see her—"

"The audacity," Sam drawls, not offended.

"—or he tries to charm his way into a meeting." I have to laugh, thinking of it. Wesson hasn't much practice in making requests either. He practically spits the word *please*.

"Perhaps he's upset that none of us know where we're going or why?" Sam muses aloud. "I don't suppose you'd care to share those details with me."

I shift uncomfortably. The truth is, Wesson *does* know exactly where we're going and why. He, the captain, Celia, and I are the only ones who do. "Sam, you know that I would if I could, but...the captain doesn't want to say anything until we know more."

She sighs, rolling her eyes. "I suppose I can understand that." She cuts a mocking glare to me. "I don't *like* it, but I understand it."

"Trust me, if things pan out as we hope—"

"Don't *tease,* Grace. It's unkind." She leans forward, peering over my shoulder. "Oh, that's no good," she murmurs. Absently, she inches the helm to the left, correcting my course, and jerks her chin toward the deck, where Wesson is busy.

I turn to see Anne down below, determinedly lugging a wooden bucket across the floor. It sloshes up and over the rim, and I wince. There's only one thing in the world with a consistency quite like that.

When he notices her, Wesson sets his mop aside for the first time since he began his task in order to watch her progress. Anne stands not two yards from him, makes eye contact, and thrusts the contents of the bucket across his freshly-swabbed deck.

My swears are echoed by Wesson's below, but both of us are nearly drowned beneath Sam's laughter.

The deck is covered in shit. I almost can't believe it, but its stench rises to invade my nostrils and testify to its presence until I shake a handkerchief free to stifle the odor. In all my days as quartermaster—as a *pirate*—I've seen many things, but nothing has filled me with quite this much incredulity.

*None shall relieve herself upon the deck. She who does shall be subject to five lashings upon her back.*

It's right there in the ship's articles. I'd always thought it ridiculous that we needed such a rule, but every time we voted, the crew was overwhelmingly in favor of keeping it on the books. And (my rotten luck), as quartermaster, it's my job to mete out the punishment.

"I await your consequences, Miss Porter!" Anne calls up to the helm, offering a sardonic salute before marching away, leaving her bucket behind.

Anne's been on the *Luck*'s crew longer than I have, and she's well-liked. And certainly, I can understand her wrath. She'd fled a violently abusive husband to join up, and we'd flouted the ship decree that had given her security that she wouldn't have to live among his kind again.

And now, I'd have to whip her for it. Gods, I'm dreading this. But our laws are clear.

"Best be off, haven't you?" Sam says, quirking an eyebrow in my direction.

I massage my temples. "I suppose I had better. Man the helm, would you?"

Below, Wesson's shoulders heave in an unmistakable sigh as he lifts the mop and begins swabbing anew.

Anne's lashes are the lightest ones I've ever delivered. But by the end of the week, as Maude, Brianna, Elinor, Katya, and Abby each take a turn spilling piss and feces across Wesson's clean deck and then lining up for their token punishment, I begin to put my back into them.

If the crew has nothing to fear from the consequences, they're more likely to flout the more serious decrees in the ship's articles. Things like *All prizes from a capture shall be declared to the quartermaster for equal distribution* or *Crew shall not steal from crew. She who commits theft against the* Luck *shall be marooned and left with a pistol loaded with a single shot.*

Everyone on-board the *Luck*, without exception, contributes.

One small blessing in all of this is Wesson's brother, little John, doesn't draw the ire of the crew the way Wesson does. Whether it's because John is so young that we're all disarmed by his innocent voice or because of his genuine sweetness, I don't know. But John's put to work running errands as the ship's newly minted cabin boy without incident. Sometimes, he runs messages from one of the ship's officers to another. Sometimes, he helps Maude in the galley or our carpenter, Jane, with her tools.

These tasks were always covered before little John's arrival, of course, but not so neatly. We'd all pitched in to handle the duties that would ordinarily be assigned to a cabin girl. We never had someone young or well-suited to the position before. Other ships would snatch up any unattended little lad to handle their menial tasks, but not us. Another rule in our ship's articles: we don't kidnap children.

And with young boys excluded from the position, there's been no one to assume its duties; there aren't many young girls lining up to join the hard life of piracy. Never mind that it's a free life. I'd come on-board the *Luck* when I was but seven years old. But then, I've been a bit of an exception to the rule.

John doesn't even ruffle feathers when he worms his way between the seat crew at meal times. If anything, they seem more amused by his antics than anything. But the amusement vanishes when his scowling brother snatches him away, squirreling them both away to eat in a corner.

Days later, despite the way he grits his teeth and gets on with his work no matter the circumstances, Wesson has done naught to endear himself to me.

"But *why* won't the captain see me?" he asks again.

"Do cease with the whining, Mr. Wesson," I say absently, steering him from the captain's cabin door for what seems like the umpteenth time. "It's quite unbecoming."

"I beg your pardon, Miss Porter. I am a nobleman," he says, affronted. "We do not whine."

"Mr. Wesson, I have yet to meet a boy, girl, woman, or man who has not, on some occasion, felt the need to whine about some perceived slight against them, some sort of inconvenience, or a minor injustice," I say. "I confess I've even whined myself on occasion. And, if anything, your sort seems even *more* greatly predisposed to it than the rest."

"I was taught never to contradict a lady," he says stiffly.

"Contradict away." I grin. "I'm no lady. Just a humble pirate."

He sighs, and I'm not sure how to interpret the sound. Perhaps he's annoyed with me. More likely, he doesn't see the sense in continuing our good-natured debate.

"You're entitled to your opinion, Miss Porter. Just as I suppose I am entitled to ignore it."

And as he rejects my opinion, *I*, for my part, choose to overlook his pouting, spoiled, *nobleman* ways. Part of the reason the crew elected me quartermaster is that I do my best to explain the reasoning behind my commands. I pretend that Wesson is just another member of my crew as I explain.

"The captain won't see you, Mr. Wesson, because she is *busy*. If we're to set upon this quest with you, there are a great many things that must be accomplished. I personally have been seeing to such tasks as counting our remaining stores, that we may be certain to obtain the proper amount once we find ourselves on Cielito. She—*we*—must carefully consider our options when asking the map to reveal its secrets. We'll have to vote as a crew which treasure we pursue, but we'll narrow down the options for voting."

There is no guilt with the knowledge that Wesson thinks himself safely a part of those treasure hunts, secure in the idea that none of us barbaric pirates could *possibly* speak the Word of the Ancient Ones. There's not even a twinge of remorse knowing that, once we obtain the map, it'll be ours and ours alone, and he and his brother will be left behind, shunted to the side.

I've already saved Wesson's life when I didn't have to. I don't owe him a thing.

I continue, "There's also the fact that it's a naval ship you've set us after."

"It was an exploratory vessel, the same as ours was, and—"

"It was a warship," I say flatly. "And we need to consider that it may well have aligned itself alongside a fleet of its countrymen."

He says nothing, choosing instead to ball his hand into a fist. Handy little tell of his. It conveys his frustration just as neatly as a scream in my face would. Gods, he's wound tighter than a spring.

"Fine," he says. "Then—" He breaks off, hissing in pain.

My eyes narrow. "And what in the Eleven Seas is wrong with you now?"

"Blisters." He unfurls his fingers to reveal the raw, ripped-open skin of his palm.

I feel a pang of empathy. They're a nasty-looking set; blood pools in his hand from the reopened wounds and drips down onto the deck, staining it.

"I'm mopping that blasted deck twice-over most days," he says angrily. And just as quickly as it visited, my sympathy flees. "My back is red and peeling and—"

"I've an ache in my neck," I interrupt. "A sea fly bit me. My ration wasn't big enough. My thirst is something powerful. The sun's too hot, the rain's too cold, and there's a pebble in my boot." If my dry tone wasn't enough to convey my annoyance with his whines, the way I advance a step closer with each false complaint must do the trick, for Wesson's mouth drops open as he retreats, staring at me, aghast, until I have him backed against the deck railing. He grasps at it with both hands for support, and a bead of blood from his blisters drips overboard.

My heart lurches in my chest. But I do my best not to betray this worry as I poke him in the chest for emphasis, delivering the end to my lesson. "Life at sea is *not* butterflies and daisies, Wesson. Her gift is freedom, but it's not something she gives for free."

He manages to fasten his jaw, looking properly chastised. "Leo," he says.

"What?" I glare up into his brown eyes.

"You don't wish to call me Lord Wesson. And I dislike being called 'Wesson.'" Here, he looks away from me and squints into the sunlight. "It...reminds me of my father." He looks down at me again and offers a rakish grin. "Call me Leo. It seems a fair compromise."

"Fine. See yourself to Jane, *Leo*." I drawl his name mockingly. "She'll give you a salve and bandages for your palms."

"Jane..." He repeats her name searchingly, and his eyes widen when he realizes who she is. "Isn't Jane the carpenter?"

"We haven't a surgeon on-board. But not to worry. She'll fix you up without driving a nail through the blisters." I smile wolfishly. "Well...unless you deserve it."

But despite my exceedingly comforting words, he looks worried. He chuckles and shoves his hands behind his back. "Oh, there's no need for that. My hands will be fine."

I snort and punch him lightly on the arm. "I'm just having a laugh, Leo. Truly, go see Jane. You don't want to risk those getting infected. I can't have you dripping blood all over the deck and into the water."

"Worried about sharks?"

"Yes." If he knew me even a little bit, he'd realize that my response is a bit too quick.

"Hmm." His gaze lingers on me for a moment, skeptical. Like he *did* catch how unnaturally fast my answer came. With startling clarity, I realize how close I still stand to him, pressing him against the railing. The ship rocks, and he grabs my waist to steady himself, not having found his sea legs quite yet.

"A bit overly familiar, aren't we now, Leo?" I drawl, using humor to break the moment, to cover the sound of my staccato heartbeat. "We only just got ourselves onto a first-name basis."

"I adapt quickly...Grace." He uses my given name, and I remove his hands from my waist as if they've burned me.

*He's bold*, I think as I step away. Too bold. He goes from spoiled weakling to something just this side of dangerous. And I'd prefer him to stay in the safe zone.

I've always been just a bit too attracted to risk.

"I'll find Jane," he says, eyes steady on mine as I take another step back, putting more distance between us. "Thank you."

"You're welcome," I say to the empty air long after he's gone.

My gaze moves to the sea below, where Leo's blood vanished into the tide, and I suppress a shudder, praying that the silver in the water is just a trick of the sunlight on the waves.

For it is decidedly *not* sharks that I'm worried about.

*From the ship's articles of the* Lady Luck*:*

*Captain and other officers shall be elected by a vote of the crew.*

# 5

When we make port in Cielito one week later, the captain is quick to delegate different tasks among the crew. Maude, Anne, and Bonnie will see to it that we have enough food, water, rum (for when the water goes stagnant), and other necessities for several more weeks at sea. Jane will obtain any tools or materials she needs to make repairs to the ship. Sam will stay with the *Luck*, and Celia and I will put our ears to the ground on the island to find out if anyone has seen our friends aboard the Tigrid warship.

Ilene looks up at me as she finishes lacing her boots. "You and Celia can go together—"

"Thank you, Captain." I cut her off. "But I think we can get more information if we work separately."

*Besides*, I finish silently, *I don't trust Celia to watch my back without sticking a knife in it.* She's had it out for me since the crew elected me first mate over her.

We board the longboats, and there's only the dip and gentle splash of the oars in the water beneath clear blue skies and an unfriendly sun as we row ashore and Cielito pulls into sharper view.

Once a colony belonging to the Allarian king (or, well, his ancestors, I suppose), it became a hub for sea trade and transport. Bars, whorehouses for sailors on leave, and all manner of supply stores sprang up as if they were daisies blooming overnight. With its convenient positioning between major land ports, but far from the reach of any law, it naturally drew attention of other...less savory characters on the Eleven Seas. Today, it's traded upon largely by pirates and a few naval officers who are willing to look the other way when they hear tales of crimes upon the high seas. And the Allarian king seems to have resigned himself to the fact that the land simply will not be governed.

Simple docks greet us as we come ashore. Things haven't changed much here, the wooden planks patchy and rotting in places. But when I swing my legs over the dock's ladder, my boots thump down upon them, as though unafraid that my feet will go straight through, splintering the wood.

I flip a coin in midair, in good spirits suddenly. Its gold

catches the light of the sun. I'll start at The Copper Ring. Nearly everyone passes through there. And nearly everyone *interesting* who passes through has a word with Jessamine.

"Grace?"

I snap to attention at Leo's uncertain voice and raise a curious brow. "Yes?"

There's a strange expression on his face, and it takes me moment to place it. Vulnerability. It doesn't look comfortable resting on Leo's features, and I find that *I'm* uncomfortable seeing him exposed like this. He motions to himself and little John, lingering in his shadow. "What are we to do?"

"That's your own concern," I say, shrugging as look away, checking my belt to ensure that my weapons and flask are in their proper positions. "Find yourself a girl, have yourself a drink... Just don't find yourself poured into a gutter when the ship pulls out."

The insecurity on his face vanishes as he grins, looking at me from beneath his lashes. "You wouldn't leave without me."

He's confident. Cocky...and *arrogant*. Foolishly so. I have to bite my tongue to hold in a laugh at his expense.

"We would," I say. My tone isn't harsh, but gentle. I'm matter-of-fact, and his smile dims. "There are other interpreters, Mr. Wesson. With the promise of untold treasures, do you imagine it would take us very long to find one?"

This is the closest I will allow myself to tell him the fate that awaits him once we find the map. The *Luck* already has her interpreter: me.

"No," he says thoughtfully. A pensive finger goes to his chin. "No, I suppose not." His eyes are somewhere very far-off, but they refocus on me decisively as he comes to some internal conclusion. "Good day, Miss Porter."

"Good day, Mr. Wesson."

He and his brother stride off into the dusty streets while the rest of the crew disappears down the island's paths, vanishing like water through a sieve. Some are headed to complete their assigned tasks, but most of them will be taking the suggestions I provided Leo. Find themselves a man or woman for a few hours, find themselves *several* drinks...and well, if there were a happy marriage of both libations *and* lust to be had, so much the better. I might just see a few of them in Jessamine's place.

Enough dawdling. I stop staring after the crew and make my way to The Copper Ring.

My coin makes a sharp plink as it bounces off an abandoned copper mug to settle upon the wooden surface. It's still spinning when it's whisked neatly from counter into an efficient fist. Jessamine's nails are tidily trimmed as her fingers close around her payment.

Her brown curls hang loosely, bound by an ineffectual blue ribbon, but Jessamine must have felt particularly determined to triumph over her hair this morning as her head is topped by a bandanna of a similar shade. She wears a light white tunic over brown breeches that meet sturdy-looking boots at her calves. Earbobs in the shape of golden hoops hang from her ears; they always do. I once heard that she wore them so your attention would be drawn to her ears, to entice you to whisper secrets into them.

I also heard once that when a man tried to grab her closer using them as a handle, she'd neatly inserted the knife she used behind the bar into his rectum. And that he'd died a slow painful death of infection.

I never heard of anyone else grabbing her hoops again.

Her welcoming smile fades to a guarded one when she looks up from her coin to see that it's me.

"Grace," she says, cordial-like. Jessamine's always polite, until someone gives her a reason not to be.

"Jess," I return.

"You paying for drink or information?"

I go for my winningest smile. "Both?"

A hard stare is my reward, and I sigh, plunking another coin down onto the counter.

She snatches it up without breaking eye contact, and

her smile relaxes into something real. There *may* have been an occasion or two in the past where I managed to draw her into casual conversation, obtaining information without truly paying for it. Today, I see, will not be a repeat of those events. "Both, it is. What'll the drink be?"

"Give me whatever you're trying to get rid of that won't poison me." A less than subtle attempt to remain on Jess's good side.

"Got a brandy that no one else seems all that taken with, if you've got the stomach for it," she says.

"Well, with *that* ringing endorsement, how could I say no?" I ask as I ease myself onto a barstool.

She vanishes for a moment, back into her stores, while the quiet conversation from the other two patrons in the bar fills the space, grunts and voices too low for me to understand what they're saying. The sea breeze rattles the bar's shutters on its windows, and I swat distractedly at a fly buzzing close, hoping for a taste of the sweat that beads down my cheeks.

Jess returns, sliding my drink across the bar, and it lands neatly in my open palm. I take a cautious taste, then another. It's not the best brandy I've ever had, but it's better than half the stuff we have on-board.

"Thank you," I say.

"No trouble. Now, what can I find for you in the way of information?"

I pause while I sip my drink, considering. Part of me thinks that I should meander my way to the question, give her some cause to think that the inquiry isn't as important as it truly is. But the larger part of me knows that Jess is too canny not to see through the roundabout path my question may take. She'll know the ask is bigger than it appears.

"Have you heard any talk of a Tigrid warship passing through? Or of anyone who ran into one?"

"Why?" she asks suspiciously. The fact that it's a warship that I'm inquiring after is enough to pique her interest. We almost never go after military vessels. They're too often well-equipped with trained fighters, better weapons, more committed zealots. It's a much smarter play to go after trading vessels than to find yourself in the midst of a war.

"I'm just...curious," I say as innocently as I can muster and drain my cup.

"Hmm. No one who ever traded me coin for rumor was ever 'just curious.'" Jessamine takes my empty glass and wipes it dry with her bar rag, a skeptical brow raised. She doesn't believe a word I'm saying. Not that I expected her to. But better she has her doubts than she knows for certain. If anyone knew we had a lead on the Map of Omna, every ship in the Eleven Seas would be on our heels, chasing after it as well.

So let her be doubtful. She can know that I'm lying; it

doesn't get her anywhere close to what the truth is. If she knew *that*, I'd be vulnerable to her next patron willing to pay for conversation.

"We stumbled upon an Allarian wreck they left behind. They decimated the poor bastards. It seemed odd that the battle was one-on-one, and neither ship was part of a larger fleet."

Her eyes narrow. "You're thinking they're protecting something?"

"I suppose I might."

She sighs, rolling her eyes. "Don't know what you and Ilene are really up to, but...all right. Let's pretend like I believe you. It may be that someone came through here a few days ago. It *may* be that they saw a ship flying Tigrid colors and sailing east."

My heart skips a beat, and I wet my lips in anticipation. "East, you say?"

"Mmhmm." She eyes me, watching my reaction. "Now, if it were *me* on a warship heading east, I'd maybe make a stop on...oh, I don't know. Cavellia? Capri di Flores?"

"You've got a sailor's instinct, Jess. I must say I think I'd do the very same." I leap from my stool, thoughts racing. I should get back to the *Luck* with this news. No. No, I need to wait until I've gone about the island, see if there's anything more. A complete report. An entire picture. *That's* what I need to bring to Captain Ilene.

The door into the tavern swings open, and Jess's attention drags from me to her new patrons. Anne, Maude, and Bonnie.

"Ladies," I greet them.

"Miss Porter," Anne returns easily, without any apparent ill will for the lashes. She nods to her companions. "We've got the supplies we need. We're just gonna have ourselves a wee drink in reward."

"Enjoy," I tell them as they take their seats at the bar. "Jessamine? Thanks."

"Grace," Jessamine calls after me, and my attention returns to her, my hand poised over the door's handle. "Your pa was in here the other day."

My speeding thoughts come to a screeching halt. The world loses color, and Jessamine's voice comes from very far away.

"He was asking after your ma," she says and tilts her head to the side. "And he asked after you, as well."

Time speeds up again, light and sound crashing into me. "Neither my mother nor I are anyone's business," I snap. "Least of all his."

And with that, I leave without even a glance behind me.

My father *had* the option to be in my life once. If he'd wanted to fight for me, I *could* have been his business.

I was seven when Captain Ilene boarded my father's

naval vessel, following a lead on the Map of Omna. She'd been quiet on the ship, living discreetly, disguised as a man with her breasts bound, hat low over her eyes, and acting the part of a common sailor.

Ilene didn't find the map on-board; she found something better.

Only the captain's wife—my mother—figured out the truth about her. And at some point, through all the secrecy and shared desires, the two of them fell in love.

It would be weeks before the *Luck*, helmed by Celia in Ilene's stead, would pull alongside my father's ship, and its crew of women would crash onto the deck in a flurry of steel and lead. I have hazy memories of clinging to my father in the melee while my mother tried to tug me free. She was so desperate to keep me with her when she followed after Ilene into the life of freedom and love she so desperately wanted.

What happened after that is a memory that is crystal clear. My father pried my fingers from his arms and flung me toward my mother.

"Take her and get off my ship," he spat at her as I wailed, kicking my legs beneath my skirts in an attempt to break free. "Women are nothing but bad luck. It was a curse to ever have you on-board."

So Ilene got us to the *Lady Luck* and we sailed away. And it was my good fortune that we did. I grew up so much more that the pussy-footed whelp that I'd been blooming into aboard the naval vessel my father had led.

And it had turned out my father was right. Women are *terrible* luck. At least, for anyone who crosses us.

I sigh, leaning against a stone wall on the streets of Cielito and thumping my fist rhythmically against its rough surface while I think. Gods, I need a drink. And I need something better than the brandy I'd let Jessamine pour down my gullet. Thankfully, there's another pub around the corner, and I have enough left in my coin purse for a pint.

When I duck into the next bar, I have to fight the instinct to groan aloud.

There, in the dank, dim light, sits Captain Whighorn. A cowering boy, younger even than John Wesson, cowers at his elbow. He winces every time Whighorn gestures, and the lad sports a deep purple eye.

The crew of the *Broken Serpent* don't share the *Luck's* qualms with kidnapping children to serve as cabin boys, forcing them into labor on-board. This tow-haired little fellow can't have been in the *Serpent's* service for long—he doesn't have a sun-burnt look to him yet. And Whighorn's brand is still fresh on his arm. A hissing snake, divided into three pieces, rears up, fangs bared, from the crook of the lad's arm. He must have struggled when they held the fiery iron to his skin; the edges are drawn wider than they should be. As if the hot metal slipped.

Whighorn and his cohorts ignore the boy, focused intently on their conversation. There are four empty glasses, I note. But only three of them. I can't imagine they allowed the boy to join them.

My eyes scan the bar, searching for their fourth companion. The last time I ran into Whighorn and his men, I nearly came to blows with them over the sneering insults they delivered. Should today prove to be a similar occasion, I want to make sure I know what I'm up against.

But I don't find a fourth member of the *Serpent*'s crew. Instead, my eyes settle on one of my own. On Celia.

Her form, lithe and full of feline grace, is unmistakable as she returns from the bar, clutching four mugs of ale.

*Four* mugs of ale.

There's no one else from the *Luck* here. But she *can't* be—

My thoughts are cut short when Celia pulls out an empty stool and settles into it, clearly the missing fourth member of Whighorn's party. Whighorn's gray beard dips into his drink as he takes a sip, and the lot of them cheer Celia's return.

This ratchets my eyebrows, already hoisted into my hairline, up yet another notch.

Whighorn is just…the worst kind of pirate. Everything he does is for sport—the killing, the slaughtering of any ship that crosses his path. It's never about a treasure waiting for him at the end of the road—though, make no mistake, he'd calmly slice the throat of a newborn if it meant it got him a twopence. It's about a lust for blood, the thrill of seeing the fear in a victim's eyes. He doesn't just take their wealth. He takes *everything*.

And he does not take women among his ranks—not that any of us would want a place there.

So what in *any* deity's name is Celia doing taking a place at his table? Much less, with her presence there being *toasted* to?

There's really no choice but for me to find out. My mouth firms with the decision, and I march straight over, dragging a chair from one of the other tables behind me and straddling it when I reach Celia, Whighorn, and his crew.

"Fancy a drink, gents?" I feign surprise when Celia glares at me. "Oh, my mistake, I should have said *lady* and gents. Celia." I nod to her. "What brings you here?"

"Same as you, Miss Porter." I know I'm not imagining the angry gravel in her normally silky purr. "Buying these fine gentlemen a drink and sharing tales of our adventures on the high seas."

She *can't* mean that she's trying to get information from these good-for-nothings?

I know that Captain Ilene expects us to get results, but

there are some lows even she wouldn't ask us to stoop to. Fraternization with the crew of the *Broken Serpent* most decidedly falls into that category.

"It's a good day when a lady wants to buy you a drink," Whighorn says in his rasp of a voice. Just the sound of it sends a shudder down my spine. "Better still when two of them do." His scraggly, unkempt beard hangs low, dripping ale onto the table's surface. He spins a rusted knife in one of the table's pockmarks and grins at me.

"I'm afraid that a mere 'good' day will have to do," Celia says, increasing the strength of her glare in my direction. "Miss Porter was *just leaving.*" Unmistakably, she widens her eyes at me and jerks her head toward the exit.

I gnaw at my tongue between my teeth, thinking it over. The captain'll have my hide if Celia tells her that I interfered in her work. Celia's here voluntarily and clearly thinks she can get information from Whighorn's lot. And her companions, in as poor taste as they may be, aren't *really* any of my business if we're not on-board the *Luck*. As we're on land...

"As the lady says," I say, standing. Whighorn's beady eyes follow me, and he licks the edge of his blade clean without taking his gaze off of me. I tilt an imaginary cap in their direction. "I must return to the *Luck*. A ship needs her quartermaster." I can't resist this jibe in Celia's direction before bidding them all adieu. "Good sailing, gentlemen."

"Good sailing, lass," Whighorn responds while one of his men simply grunts something unintelligible at me.

I leave the bar, their voices dropping behind me to continue discussing their business as I make my exit, bumping into Anne, Maude, and Bonnie as I leave. I mumble some apology for the collision and continue on my way, my feet meandering through the streets of Cielito back to the docks and the longboats. I board one of them to make my merry way back to the *Luck*, and my mind sifts through everything I've seen and heard today. If Jessamine is to be believed, we're bound for Cavellia and Capri di Flores next. My absentee father has taken a sudden, inexplicable interest in me, and *Celia* is on friendly terms with *Whighorn*.

It's this last thought that gnaws on me, and I turn it over and over again—like a locked puzzle box that I can't find the answer to.

Lost in my worries, it doesn't hit me until I set foot back on the *Luck*: I never did get that second drink I wanted.

Parry. Parry. Thrust.

Beneath a blanket of crystal-clear stars, Captain Ilene forces my movements across the deck, our weapons clanging as they meet for each strike. She feints, and I have to scramble to block the real attack.

Though I'm trying, my thoughts aren't as focused on the duel as they should be. I can't stop thinking about Whighorn and Celia. Celia and Whighorn.

I grimace, the image of his gold-capped teeth and mean little eyes swimming before me. Ilene had seemed satisfied with my report from Jessamine and undisturbed when I casually mentioned running into Celia with the *Serpent*'s crew. But I can't help how it gnaws at me.

I'm sure Ilene's composure would have been shaken if I had mentioned my father and his interest in my mother. Nothing gets to Ilene quite like the reminder that my mother had a love life before her—much less someone who is her opposite in nearly every way: gender, an upstanding member of society...

Hastily I block another of Ilene's strikes, but she returns faster than I am prepared for and sends my sword sailing across the deck.

She claps my shoulder and gestures to a bench. "Not your finest work, Gracie."

I'm forced to agree as I take my seat and swipe my arm across my forehead to wipe away the perspiration beaded there. Even without giving the duel all of my attention, battling Captain Ilene isn't for the faint of heart. "That it wasn't."

"Don't be too hard on yourself." She grins and, after

taking a swig for herself, hands me a waterskin. "There will be plenty more chances for you to try and best me when we're en route to Cavellia and Capri di Flores.

I sip at the water and, *gods*, it's fresh. It hasn't turned rancid from standing in a barrel yet. That's one of the few things I miss about land when we're long at sea. And one of the few reasons I look forward to returning to port. I pass the waterskin back to her.

"Captain..." I hesitate to ask. "After Cavellia and Capri di Flores, once we have the map in our possession...where will we go next? What will we ask it for?"

She eyes me curiously. "Well, now, that's up to the crew, isn't it? We'll put it to a vote, as we always do."

"Yes, of course," I agree hastily. "But won't we present them with some guidance? A few choices?"

She sighs and takes a gulp of water before sheathing her cutlass. "I sense you're not asking without reason. Am I right?" When I don't answer, she sighs again and shakes her head. "All right, Gracie, I'll play your game. Yes. We'll give them choices. And the option I plan to make a case for is La Isla de Oro.

A wave of dismay washes over me. The Island of Gold would be a hard prize to pass up. The land is another presumed myth, where the leaves are precious metals and the trees are populated with berries in the form of rubies, emeralds, and sapphires. Where the rivers flow molten gold. Where the squawk of a bird overhead is accompanied by the screech of its silver feathers scraping together with every flap of its wing.

La Isla de Oro doesn't have a hidden treasure. It *is* the hidden treasure.

Without any water to drink or food to hunt or gather, you may easily die upon its shores...but you'd die rich.

Still...it *is* a myth. There's no proof that it's real. Not like the Mordgris. Every member of our crew knows of their existence, can share at least one story wherein their face grows white in the recounting of the tale. A great many of them still shake when I mention my mother. They'd seen her struggling in the Mordgris' grip, trying to return to me.

Before I lose myself in the memory, I fight my way back to the present moment. "La Isla de Oro may not exist," I say.

"Maybe not," she agrees. "And if the Map of Omna tells us it doesn't, or if the crew doesn't vote to pursue it, we'll move on to the next thing. But the map seems to exist. Why not this, too? And if it *does* exist, then, Gracie..." The captain's eyes glimmer in avarice. "I just don't see how that's a chance that we can let go."

I fear that she's right. What pirate in her right mind could overlook such a gift? And yet...

I strive to remain nonchalant. "I thought of an option

myself."

"Oh?" She cocks an inquisitive brow, inviting me to elaborate.

"I thought the crew might be interested in finding the home of the Mordgris."

Her head jerks up, expression painted with horror. "*No.*"

The instant refusal, the denial without even pretending to humor my suggestion, raises my hackles just as quickly. "It's not about—"

"I said, *no*, Grace. We're *not* going after Helen."

"What about the treasure they're said to guard?" I ask furiously, ignoring the way my pulse jumps at my mother's name. "What of the fact that it's tied to their power? We could rid the sea of their presence forever and become rich women in the process. You're telling me the crew would just want to blindly reject that opportunity? Two bounties for the price of one."

"The Mordgris do not trade in gold," she fires back. "They trade in flesh and blood, souls and *darkness*, Grace. In *death*. Do you truly think that any treasure they guard won't come at a great price?"

"I think it's up to the crew to decide if it's a price they're willing to pay." I'm nearly vibrating with suppressed anger. The crew can have the treasure. I could care less about it. I want to destroy those wretched creatures. And if it comes at a cost of giving up my bounty, so be it.

The fight goes out of her suddenly, and she slumps, looking tired, defeated, as old as I've ever seen her. "Deny it all you want," she says, shaking her head. "But this is about your mother. It's always about her."

"*Of course it is!*" I cry. I rake a frustrated hand through my hair and look down at the deck, fighting back stinging tears. "Of course it is," I repeat, quieter this time.

My eyes snap to Ilene's. "The map could lead us to her— or at the very least to avenge her. You're supposed to have loved her," I say. "Why isn't it always about her for *you,* too?"

Shocked into silence, her mouth opens and closes wordlessly. She sighs and pushes to her feet, beginning to walk away, before changing her mind. A gentle hand smooths over my hair, and she presses a kiss to my temple.

"Helen is gone," she says. "But I miss her, too, Gracie."

I close my eyes and listen to the sound of her boots retreating. "They have to come from somewhere," I say, throat clogged with emotion. My voice isn't loud, but in the stillness of the night air, I know it carries easily to her ears. Her strides halt. "I'm going to find them. Find them— and destroy them."

After another moment, she has no response. Her footsteps resume, carrying her away.

I don't know how much longer I sit there. It could be

minutes. It could be hours.

When I open my eyes, the sky hasn't grown any darker or lighter, but I snap to alertness at the sound of my name. *Grace.*

I follow the call, finding my way up to the forecastle. Before looking overboard, I brace myself, knowing what I'll see. This isn't the first time they've summoned me like this.

My mother's face bobs in the water.

Despite expecting it, seeing her knocks the breath from me. Her eyes are exactly the same: that unearthly teal, spotted with dark flecks. Her hair is sodden, slicked back and billowing about her shoulders on the tide. It's cruel, how healthy she looks. She's just as I remember her, down to the small beauty mark above her lip.

She tilts her head to the side. "Oh," she sighs in that musical way she always had. "Gracie."

My hands knot themselves around the railing, drinking in the sight of her.

A second form breaks the surface, and a strangled sound leaves my throat. My mother's twin.

"Grace." When *she* smiles at me, it's needle-sharp.

Another face rises above the water. "Gracie."

Another. "Grace."

Soon, I have seven mothers bobbing in the sea's embrace. They chant my name, repeating *Gracie-Grace-Gracie-Grace-Grace-Grace* over and over and *over* again, like a flock of gulls, their voices—my *mother's* voice—growing higher and more mocking with every utterance.

This is one of the Mordgris' cruelest tricks. They wear the form of someone you love, and they torture you with it.

It's too much. This isn't the first time, but it's worse every time. There are *more* of them every time. And with each appearance, they grow bolder and bolder, getting increasingly close to the ship.

I swallow a hysterical lump in my throat and yank my pistol from my belt with shaking hands, firing haphazardly into the water. I'm usually a good shot, but can't bring myself to aim at my mother's face. I miss by a wide margin, the shot plinking harmlessly into the waves.

They finally abandon the illusion, my mother's face vanishing into the all-too-familiar visage of the Mordgris. Gray skin stretched tight over a noseless skull, pointed teeth stretched wide in seven grins below inky eyes.

"Good night, Gracie," they hiss in tandem. Their heads sink beneath the waves.

My gun swings up for a second shot, but before I can fire, their silver tails vanish below the surface.

"Grace?"

I wheel around, pistol still outstretched, and a wide-eyed Leo ducks beneath my range, immediately holding up his hands in surrender.

"Sorry," I gasp, as winded as if I'd just swam leagues. "I'm... Sorry." Hastily, and hoping that he doesn't notice how my hands still tremble, I holster the gun.

"What in the king's name are you firing at?" he asks, sounding bewildered. He cautiously lowers his hands and steps closer to me, keeping a wary eye on the pistol at my hip.

"Just...target practice." Instantly, I want to bite back the words. Target practice? At what, the waves? I couldn't have said that I was cleaning the gun instead?

"Right," Leo says, his voice conveying every drop of his doubt. Still, bless him, he doesn't prod me any further.

I change the subject hastily. "Didn't take you much for a life at sea. Thought you would have taken every last second you could ashore. What brought you back?"

"Ah. Well..." He rocks back on his heels, considering his response. "As inappropriate as the island was for John's impressionable eyes in the daylight, Cielito only worsened as the hour grew late. We waited by the longboats until some of your crew wished to return. Once John had eaten, I saw him to bed, but I found myself too restless to do the same."

"Did the two of you have yourselves a pleasant day?" I ask absently, scanning the waves for any sign of the Mordgris.

"Well..." I glance back to see him turning out his empty pockets. "No one much cared to lend me any coins, never mind that I assured them my family fortune was safe at the

Wesson estate and they would be rewarded for any generosity. So John and I simply walked about. We seized the opportunity to have stillness beneath our feet."

"You're lucky no one snatched you," I admonish. "Be smart. Don't go flashing your title about. An idiot may get it into their head that someone would pay a pretty penny for your safe return." I cut him a wry look. "Of course, if they knew how irritating you could be, they'd likely give you back."

A winning smile is flashed at me, a burst of brightness among the dark. Suddenly, I'm thankful that it's night. For the moon and stars alone aren't enough to betray the heat rising in my cheeks.

"But they *would* pay a pretty penny," he says. "The *prettiest* penny. But still not as pretty as you, Miss Grace."

"Flatterer." His smiles may disarm me, but the compliment rolls right off.

He shrugs, not offended. "One can try." His eyes sweep the deck. "You're alone up here?"

I raise a brow. "Do you see someone else I ought to know about?"

"No. It's just... I thought I heard another voice."

I blanch. He heard them then—the Mordgris. I wouldn't mind him knowing that the creatures are *here*. But I don't wish to share their particular affinity for me, how they taunt me with my mother's form. These moments, strange as they are, are mine and mine alone. I greedily hoard any memories of my mother's face—even when it's not her wearing it.

So instead of telling Leo the truth, I say, "Oh, that was just me, myself, and I. Thinking out loud."

The quirk of his lips makes his eyes dance, and I find I have to look to the sea once more. "And what are the three of you thinking about?"

Here, I decide to be honest. "My mother."

"Ah." He eases himself next to me. "Left her behind to pirate, did you?"

I shift, uncomfortable. He's so very off-base. I didn't leave my mother. *She* left *me*. "Not exactly," I say, feeling the edge of her compass in my pocket, acutely aware of its presence against my thigh. "She was...taken from me."

"Oh." My gaze doesn't leave the ocean, but he's close enough, his arm just brushing mine, that I can feel his body tense at my words. "I'm sorry."

I jerk my head in a nod. "Thanks."

There's silence a moment longer while my hands clench the railing, hoping that he'll move on from the subject.

"You loved her, didn't you?"

The surprise in his voice tears my attention from the waves, and I look at Leo, dumbfounded. "She was my *mother.*"

"I know that."

"Then...?"

He scuffs his foot against the deck, but doesn't have the cowardice to look away from me. "You're...pirates," he says, shrugging.

"And?" I cross my arms, waiting for him to go on.

"And all we ever hear of pirates are the atrocities your kind commit. Theft, death..."

"We're still human. We laugh. We cry. We love."

"I see that now. But it would be easier if I could still think of you as a heartless lot."

He means to keep us in a little box in his mind. It's simpler to keep a distance from the idea of a villainous pirate rather than a flesh-and-blood *person.*

My eyes sweep his noble form. "I couldn't agree more," I say. Leo has proven himself a bit more than the stuck-up, spoiled brat I'd taken him for.

And, more than that, it would be far easier if I could lock my heart away and keep it shut, far away from any decisions. It would be far easier if my feelings didn't interfere. But they do. And it's those same feelings that I wish I could keep chained up that keep pushing me toward my determination to end the Mordgris.

"And what did your father have to say about all of the pirating?" He nudges my shoulder gently with his. His voice softens. "And about the loss of your mother, no less?"

I bark out a bitter laugh. "My father..." I shake my head. "He's of no importance. Besides, I'm more interested in *your* father. Tell me about the late Lord Wesson."

A dark shadow passes over his face. "I don't want to talk about him."

Curious. I tilt my head, taking in his suddenly tense posture, and open my mouth to prod a bit further. But Leo's attention is drawn down below when we both hear a splash.

Peering over the rail, he asks, "Just a fish, I'm sure?"

Below his feigned nonchalance are hope and trepidation, vying for dominance. But I see no reason to hide the presence of the Mordgris. He doesn't need to know how they toy with me—*no one* needs to know that— but it's better for him to be on his guard, knowing that they're around.

"Mordgris," I respond.

Leo's response is instantaneous, tension threading its way through his form as he stiffens. He is, no doubt, remembering the night he met them. The night he met me.

"Mordgris." He rolls the word on his tongue like a wine, as though he is trying to detect each of its notes. "I always thought they were a myth until I found myself facing them on the open sea."

"I believe most on land do. But we find ourselves in uncharted territory, chasing after omnipotent maps, encountering creatures that haunt the seas... Myths and legends seem to be coming to life before our very eyes, don't they?"

He's quiet in the face of this observation. "I suppose you're right."

His tone is soft and a bit resigned. Guilt twists my gut over being the one to pull the veil from his vision, but it's better for his eyes to be well and truly open. Only, I feel as though I've taken something from him. His sense of security, like a blanket wrapped around a small child. To mask my remorse, I clap him on the back. "No sense in dwelling on it. Get yourself to bed. If we're bringing things to life, mayhap you'll dream a dream into truth."

He manages a twisted mockery of a smile. "Actually, I'd prefer my dreams stay in sleep's realm. But you're right. It's late. Good night, Grace."

"Good night, Leo."

I watch him leave, about to return my attention back to the stars and their pinprick reflections in the waves when he pauses at the bottom of the stairs.

"Grace?" He hesitates. "I hope you won't take it as an insult if I say that the circles under your eyes are quite...dark. You ought to get some sleep soon as well."

He's right. The fatigue weighs on my shoulders, like hands pressing me toward the ground, a gravedigger determined to bury me.

Still…sleep is easier said than done. My attention drifts to the empty waves, and I wipe futilely at the ship's railing. Just in case it's blood that I cannot see summoning the Mordgris.

The wind in my ears as I head for my cabin whispers. *Graaace.*

*From the ship's articles of the* Lady Luck:

*All prizes from a capture shall be declared to the quartermaster for distribution.*

# 6

In a few days' time, we've loosed our sails, hoisted our anchor, and left Cielito at our stern. Before leaving, when the captain and I finally shared the news of our quest with the crew, we were met with murmurs of anticipation. They're all aquiver with excitement, talk of treasure and the wishes the gold could grant sweeping the crew.

The Wesson boys become the subjects of gratitude for bringing us this chance. Even Anne and her cohorts have stopped throwing shit about.

Sam swings her legs over the *Luck*'s side, carefree and smiling as she tilts her face into the sun's warmth. "What'll you do with your share?" she asks.

My mind flits once again to the idea of slaying the Mordgris. "Suppose it depends on what it's a share of," I say, striving to sound aloof and unconcerned.

She shoots me a funny look. "It's a share of *treasure*, Grace. What else would it be?"

A share of slain Mordgris. I allow myself to daydream, imagining the familiar squelching sound of my blade thrusting into flesh. Only this time, it isn't human blood I spill, but a vulnerable Mordgris, their treasure safely in our hold. I imagine avenging my mother—or better still, *finding* her, closing my eyes as she wraps me in her embrace.

I'm not sure I'm successful in hiding the flare of victory in my chest when I say, "Right. You're right, of course. Just...you know. There's a lot of treasure out there. I only wonder which we'll go after first."

She picks at something left behind in her teeth and flicks it overboard. "Don't much matter to me. Gold is gold." She grins widely and opens shining eyes. "And when we find the map, there's a whole wide world of it to find."

She's right. Riches are riches. But, regardless of what Ilene thinks, an enemy is an enemy. Whether they're made from flesh and blood or stolen souls and darkness. Everyone has a weakness. We just need to find theirs.

I bump Sam's elbow with mine. "Forget what I'd do. What will you do with *your* share?"

"Me?" She blinks. "Well, I expect I'd start with getting good and stinking drunk to celebrate. Probably find myself a good man or woman to lay with for the night." Here, she winks. "Whichever's more cost-effective. Just because I'm going to be rich doesn't mean I need to be financially irresponsible."

I laugh softly under my breath. "No, we wouldn't want that."

"My share's not equal to what you or the captain would get, of course," she says. "But I expect that after three really *big* takes, I'll finally have enough to buy a ship and lead my own crew. I fancy being a captain someday and well...with you, Celia, and Captain Ilene on-board, I don't stand much of a chance of being voted into the position here."

*That* surprises me, and I whip my head around to face her. "You'd leave the *Luck*?" I ask, incredulous. I can't fathom the idea. The *Luck* is home. The crew is family.

Her swinging feet go suddenly still, sensing my tone. Sam knows how I feel about this ship. "Yeah," she says carefully. "I would."

"Wh—"

"My position on-board *Luck* is better than any I've ever had," she says. "Trust me, it's a blessing not to have to bind my breasts for a life at sea. But this ship isn't perfect, Grace. There are things that go on amongst the crew...things you don't see."

I straighten, both alarmed and insulted. I *should* see them. I'm the quartermaster. It's my *job*. "What things?"

It's her turn to laugh. "I'm no rat. If I tell you, the next thing I know, you'll be dragging her to the cat o' nine tails. Then everyone will know I squawked, and on ship or off, my future's shot once word gets out. Not a sailor worth her salt will trust me."

I deflate. She has a point. "Ah-ha!" I say, shooting her a rueful grin and wagging a finger in her direction. "But you've given it away. Now, I know it's a 'her.'"

She laughs, long and loud, and shakes a dramatic fist in my direction. "Damn you, Grace Porter. You've pried it out of me."

"I'm a master of interrogation," I say, buffing my nails against my chest. "What can I say?"

She claps me on the back and pulls her legs onto the deck. "I'm off for the mess, Interrogation Master. I expect Rae will be down from the crow's nest any moment now, wanting me to take my shift. I'd rather do it with something in my stomach."

But alas, Sam doesn't get the chance for even a bite. No sooner have the words left her mouth than Rae's raspy yell washes over all of us, loud enough to reach those of us above and below deck. "*Shiiiiiip!*" she shouts. "There's another ship off the *Luck's* starboard!"

Half the crew scrambles to the deck. Some squint determinedly at what looks like clouds on the horizon. Others pass a spyglass around to bring the ship's sails into focus.

Quietly, I bring my own spyglass to my eye and wait for the ship to drift closer. It's a trading vessel, no doubt about that. But what are they trading?

Already, I feel the rush, the thrill that comes before seizing a new prize racing through my blood. Distantly, I hear Captain Ilene give the orders that have us picking up speed. Before long, we'll be drawing even with the merchant vessel.

The crew is a pack of eager animals, waiting to pounce on their prey, and among the commotion, Leo threads his way through the crowd with John in tow. "Is it them?" he asks, eagerness in his voice. "The Tigrid rebels?"

"No," I say, all business as I tuck my spyglass away. "Just a trade ship."

"Then, what...?" His voice trails off, clearly not liking the possible answers to his unasked question. I can read the apprehension written across his face as if it were a book.

John is just the opposite, eager and tugging his brother's sleeve determinedly. "Leo, I want to go down by Maude, I want to *see*—"

"Hush, now," Leo says, tugging his shirt loose from the boy's grip. John pouts, muttering under his breath, but his big brother ignores him. I bite back a smile at his disgruntled murmurs. Leo's eyes search mine, looking for some reassurance that he doesn't find. "What's happening exactly?"

His face tells me that he already knows, but wishes he didn't. It tells me he's praying I'll contradict what his instincts and every lick of common sense that he possesses is screaming at him.

"Why, Mr. Wesson," I drawl. "I do believe the fair sea has granted us a gift."

His gaze drifts toward the trading vessel. Poor lamb. He's beginning to look a little sick. "And that gift is...?"

"Well, it's hard to say." I let the smile unfurl like a sail catching the wind. "After all, we haven't unwrapped it yet."

Leo hauls a furious John belowdecks. The lad kicks and screams the entire way, simply furious about it, but Leo is determined. And for as much as the crew holds no love for the elder Wesson, no one is keen to force the little one into lead and bloodshed over a hope for gold.

But that doesn't change the fact that bodies on-board the *Luck* contribute. Leo will be expected to board the trading vessel with the rest of us. Fair is fair and cleaning duty only goes so far. Leo looks nauseated at the prospect and protests, but once he's resigned himself, he tucks John in with a whispered, "I'll split my share with you, all right?"

It clearly is *not* all right. Not with John, and the way it looks to sit with Leo, I'm mildly impressed he hasn't yet spilled his breakfast across the deck. Once back at the ship's rail, he extends an expectant hand. "I'll be needing a weapon."

"So you will."

"I'd prefer a pistol."

I snort. "And I, Mr. Wesson, would prefer that a unicorn prance onto the deck of the *Luck* shitting gold. But we'll both have to settle for something lesser." I hand him a cutlass, an inferior scrap of metal, poorly balanced with spots of rust. But it's what we have, so he'll need to make do.

Leo's lip curls in distaste as he tests its heft in his palm and tuts under his breath.

"I can't possibly be expected to *use*—"

"You prefer remaining alive, I assume?" I cut in.

Growing pale, he nods.

"Good. As do I. I expect nothing of you, Mr. Wesson. But I suggest that if you want to retain the breath in your lungs, you start expecting a great deal more of yourself. Including—" I nod to the cutlass "—acquainting yourself intimately with the weapon you've been granted, whether or not it is a poor substitute for the weapon you wish you had."

The merchant vessel is not filled with idiots, but they aren't equipped to fend off a crew of pirates storming their ship. As we draw even with them, our cannons are quiet. Theirs are nonexistent, only a few naval officers assigned to help defend them. Many of their crew is assembled on the deck, pistols firing wildly in the direction of the *Lady Luck*. They don't have the advantage of multiple battles under their belts or the discipline of past target practice. Still, though most of their attempted shots run wild into the wind, a couple strike true.

Next to me, Celia hisses in pain as a bullet clips her shoulder. It's merely a graze, though. She ignores the wound, calmly raises her pistol, squints her eyes in concentration, and picks out a target. There's a loud bang beside me. A blood-curdling screeching across the water. And a body hits the waves.

Celia smiles and blows at the tip of her gun, the red, healing edge of a new tattoo on her peering out from below her sleeve. "And just yesterday I was lamenting the fact that I'd been remiss in my target practice," she says.

Captain Ilene gives her an indulgent smile. "Enough showing off, Celia."

The Captain will humor Celia like this, but if I was in charge, I'd have much sharper words for her. I won't deny that I thrill at the chase of another ship, at the discovery of treasure. But it's different with Celia. Like Whighorn, she relishes the kill.

Leo swallows behind me, nervous. "What now?"

Sam shrugs. "What else?"

"Captain?" My voice is low, waiting for the order.

She grins. "Take it."

Planks are thrown from our ship to theirs, and like animals loosed from a cage, we storm our way across. My cutlass is in my right hand, my pistol in my left, and I'm over the plank before I know it, ignoring the Mordgris that have appeared to swim below, awaiting any carnage that may fall their way. They're alone in the waters. Even sharks dare not tempt a horde of hungry Mordgris.

My sword cuts a wide swath across the deck. The first brave merchant to storm my way is inexperienced, armed with a kitchen knife. I'm not without pity. I can be merciful. After all, the captain rarely means "take the *ship*" when she says "take it." It's only treasure we're after. She's no wish to split her crew. These poor saps can keep their vessel. They're welcome to sail to shore and find a safe harbor if they give us what we're after.

My cutlass swings true, cutting my opponent off at the wrist, and he screams, blood spurting from the wound as he clutches his mutilated arm.

I can't help but roll my eyes a bit. There's no need for his hysterics. As long as they have a surgeon on-board—

and if that surgeon hasn't been slain by one of my crew—his wound won't be fatal.

I open my mouth, intending to question the poor soul as he writhes around on the ground, clutching his wrists and whimpering a plea for mercy.

If he'd only hush for a moment, I'd be happy to grant his request. I fight off a spurt of annoyance. But I haven't the time to ask him what his ship carries, what the quickest route to the cargo may be.

One of the ship's naval officers rushes forward, a bayonet's point heading unerringly for me. Our weapons clang as I knock it aside, but he proves quick to recover, dropping the bayonet and pulling his own sword from its sheath.

I smile.

At last, a challenge.

My feet slide forward across the deck, testing the officer's response, and instantly, he shifts back, guard up. He matches me, strike for strike, thrust for thrust. I lunge. He blocks. But even still, I press my guard forward, my blade increasing its pressure against his, and he grits his teeth, returning the attack.

"I'm not sure which to be more insulted by," he grunts out. His face is red with effort, perspiration streaking down his face. "That I must put the skills taught to me by the king's own navy against a *pirate*—"

He spits the word, but I'm not fussed, accustomed to the distaste he shows. It's typical from those who consider themselves "civilized."

"Or," he continues on, "that said pirate is a *woman* who thinks herself my equal."

That does it for me. No matter how many times I hear that a woman is lesser, it never fails to raise my ire. Insult me for being a pirate, if you wish, but we on the *Luck* chose this life. We *didn't* choose to be women.

Still...given the option, I'd pick both. Over and over again.

"It's a tough decision. I'll give you that, sir," I pant out, increasing the pressure of my sword on his. "But—"

My leg sweeps out, hooking his ankle around my own, and he is sent sprawling across the deck below me. His shock barely has a chance to register before my cutlass's tip is at his throat. He scrambles backward, trying to get his legs back under him, but it's no good. The deck is alive, swarming with people, and he has no room to retreat.

"Your strength may be greater than mine," I tut. "But it's your bravado, sir, that deserves the real award."

I waste no more time with petty words. This challenge is over. The victor, clear. I slice cleanly across the naval officer's neck, and his eyes lose some of their pretty blue sheen as his body falls to the planks below, blood leaking from his neck like teardrops.

I lean close, mesmerized by the blood's sheen. The way the red is so dark it's almost black. The way it catches the light like the black of a Mordgris's eye. The way it sings as it falls to the deck, the splash like the burst of music and—

I shake my head, the sound of battle rushing back and covering the blood's song. What *was* that?

Nothing. It was nothing. Just the adrenaline of battle. Nothing more. I tear my eyes away from the naval officer's vacant stare and back to the assault. Our victory is nearly sealed, the merchants on the defense, most of them backed into a corner.

Even Leo has managed to do his part. He claimed that he was better with a pistol, and perhaps that's the truth, but he's no slouch with a blade either. He holds it like one who has trained with it. His other arm—the one that isn't his sword arm—hangs at his side, pressed into his side to staunch the flow of blood. He's been injured, but he seems to have taken it all in stride.

There's something in him right now... He enjoys this. He's come alive in the heat of battle, easily fending off those who rush at him. With little bloodshed, he disarms them neatly, ending their combat before it has a chance to start.

He's corralled those he's disarmed into a corner of the deck, away from the melee, and as I draw closer, I hear him speaking to them calmly.

"—to worry. My captain will be wanting to speak with you, is all."

I raise a brow. *His* captain now, is it?

"Indeed she will be, Mr. Wesson." I clap him on the shoulder, mouthing, *Well done.* He accepts the silent praise with a slight incline of his head.

I nod at a man who is clutching the symbol of his gods between gnarled fingers. "You there," I say. He gulps when my focus turns to him. "What manner of goods do you carry?"

"We're a simple transport vessel, ma'am. Paid by a great many merchants to move their goods."

He can't help the tremble that sneaks into his voice, and I tap my fingers at my hip impatiently. His eyes flick to their movement and back to mine, shuddering. Willfully, I command my fingers to still. The visage of a bloodthirsty pirate before the poor man won't encourage him to speak any quicker.

"That's good to hear," I say, hoping I strike the balance between patient and stern. More flies with honey, than vinegar after all. "And what goods might you be moving today?"

"Spices, ma'am, bolts of cloth...things of that ilk."

My heart leaps. I couldn't have asked for better if I'd written to the gods of thieves and seas themselves. Chests of gold and jewels are rarely the cargo we encounter on any vessel. But bolts of cloth…spices…those will fetch a pretty price in any port. And with this many people on-board, I'd be willing to bet that their stores of medicine and foodstuffs are aplenty. Enough to shore up our own, that's for certain.

"—I *asked* you *where*."

In the wake of battle, the thump of a boot into a vulnerable stomach and the cry of pain that follows draws my attention. I turn to see Celia standing menacingly over one of the crew members.

My captive's eyes have grown wide, and he shrinks away from me.

Leo's brow furrows, the light of battle fading from his eyes and melting into concern. He reaches for my wrist. "Grace…"

"I'll handle it," I snap, my eyes already searching for the captain. Really, she should be the one to stop Celia before things get out of hand. Celia doesn't respect my authority. She never has.

But the captain is busy on the quarterdeck, knotting ropes around the wrists of one of the remaining naval officers. In fact, she doesn't seem to have noticed anything amiss at all.

"*Ridiculous* waste of space, taking up perfectly good air that the rest of us could be using." Celia huffs impatiently and draws her sword free.

*"Grace."* Leo's tone is urgent now, and he pulls his own sword, starting in the direction of Celia and her victim, but I block his path bodily.

"I said that I would handle it, Leo," I say lowly. I keep my hands on his wrists and my eyes on his until he lowers his weapon, looking at me with guarded eyes. "This is crew business, Mr. Wesson. You're not to interfere. Watch these gentlemen and I'll be back." I gulp and gird my loins, striding briskly across the deck and leaving Leo and the crew members behind me in my shadow.

*"Celia,"* I call.

Without breaking eye contact, her sword remains poised above the crewman's throat. "Yes, Miss Porter?" she smoothly responds.

The crewman's groin is dark, and it's not from blood or sea. She's terrified the poor bastard so that he's pissed himself in the face of her and her sword, like she's the specter of death herself.

"Trouble here?" I ask, acting lofty and as though I barely notice the man on his knees before us.

"Not a whit," she answers. "I asked this man a simple question. He has, as yet, failed to deliver a satisfactory answer, proving himself *useless.*" This, she hisses out between her teeth, and I try not to betray the lump in my throat. "I thought to deliver the Mordgris a snack, save his crewmates the trouble of towing his—" her lips curve "—

*dead* weight. And then," she chirps, suddenly cheery, "I thought I'd move on to the next sailor, in hopes that they'd prove more cooperative." She raises an eyebrow at me. "Is there a problem?"

"Celia." I drop my voice. "The poor idiot is terrified. Look at him. He's been struck dumb with fear. It's no wonder he can't answer you."

The man's eyes are wide, focused solely on the tip of Celia's sword. The point of it reflects in his irises, like a hypnotist's subject, mesmerized by the object. He follows every tiny movement it makes.

She tuts. "You're right."

Before I can stop her, she lunges, drawing a startled cry from me as she severs the man's windpipe and he falls to the ground.

The men around her look shocked. One of them leans to the side, emptying the contents of his stomach onto the deck, and Celia smiles. "It's always best to put a dumb animal out of its misery."

My eyes meet Leo's horrified expression across the deck. He was beginning to look at me like he knew me. Or as if he'd like to. But now...now, he looks like he wishes he didn't know me at all. He looks like he wishes he'd never met a pirate like me.

The sound of a fired shot draws my attention back to Celia, her smoking pistol aimed toward the sky.

If there was anyone's attention that she didn't have, she has it now.

Her eyes scan over the assembled sailors, and she raises her voice. "Now, then. I *do* hope one of you can help me with my questions."

There is a crash of sound as volunteers raise their hands.

*From the ship's articles of the* Lady Luck*:*

*The business dealings of the* Lady Luck *may take place upon land. But discussion of ship business shouldn't extend beyond those on-board.*

# 7

Once the merchant sailors show us to their cargo hold, we transfer our bounty from their ship to ours with minimal aggravation.

The death of the sailor at Celia's hands still troubles me, but I try not to betray those feelings, keeping a blank expression upon my face and going about my work without speaking of it.

*After all, what right do I have to criticize her?* I rationalize as I pass a bolt of cloth to Anne. *It's not as if I haven't also taken a life today.*

It's different though, a voice inside me insists. That naval officer would have killed you. *Celia's* victim had already surrendered.

The voice sounds annoyingly like Leo. Even in the short time I've known the young Lord Wesson, he's managed to worm his way into my mind. Which I most decidedly do *not* need. Noble morality has no place onboard a pirate ship.

When we return to the *Luck*, an excitable John is there to greet us. "Well?" he prompts eagerly. His greedy eyes rake over his brother's blood-soaked form, the arm he holds stiffly at his side, and they light in anticipation. "How did it go?"

Leo's eyes drift to mine, but he says nothing. Waiting, perhaps, to see if I will deem the excursion a success. Reserving his judgement on me until then.

Unnerved by his quiet—the boy is *never* quiet—I avoid his gaze. "You'll want to find Jane," I say quietly. "See about bandaging that arm or something."

Still without a word, he uses his good arm to steer John toward the stairs and descends belowdecks. Whether it's to find Jane or collapse into his bed, I don't know.

John goes where his older brother bids, casting a curious glance back at me. But the obedience doesn't hinder him from peppering Leo with questions. His words disappear as they vanish, though the sound of his voice echoes in my ears for some time.

Once the treasure is safely stowed away, the crew splits across the deck, making their way to the different tasks needed for us to set sail. Others—those not on shift—make their way to their bunks to rest or to retrieve their own special flasks. But not Celia. She heads for our small gullery to send a message.

My eyes follow her. It's not for the first time that I wonder who it is that she's writing to. Her letter-writing habit has certainly increased as of late. I'd seen her sending a seagull off three or four times since the Wessons came on board.

So far as I know, Celia hasn't got any family that she bothers to keep in touch with. A lover, then? Perhaps. But while it wouldn't shock me to learn that she'd taken up with someone while in port, Celia is hardly what one would call sentimental. I have trouble entertaining the idea that she's sending sweet love notes back to shore.

I shake my head, lobbing my idle wondering away. What do I care if Celia's got a beau? I should be raising a glass over the triumph of my crew.

That night, there is a great deal of celebrating. The liquor on-board the merchant vessel provided us with such a surplus that the crew feels comfortable indulging in our own rations extra that evening.

Everyone turns out. The helm is manned in shifts, Jane comes above deck, and Maude leaves the galley. Lila and her gunners enjoy a drink. Sam mingles with the crew; Ilene makes the rounds; and Celia, Bonnie, and Anne find a comfortable seat in the revelry.

Well...I suppose I *should* say every member of the crew turns out. Because the Wessons are notably absent from the festivities. I haven't heard a peep from them since they went below.

"First, we sell this bounty off," Anne says. I swill my drink, watching her with Celia and Bonnie. "And then, it's onto the map."

Celia grins, raising her glass in a toast.

I cut my eyes away. Despite our good fortune, I don't feel much like celebrating. When I watch Celia, I'm thinking of Leo. Seeing us through his eyes. And I don't much care for the vision.

"Grace?" Sam's boots appear in my line of sight, below my bowed head. Her toe nudges mine. "It was a good day. You could look happier about it."

I twirl my finger in a sardonic circle. "Yippee," I say dryly.

Her brow furrows and she opens her mouth to ask what bug has crawled up my ass, but I hold up a hand. "Sorry. I'm sorry. Don't worry about me, Sam. I'm fine."

I toss the rest of my drink back and head for my bunk.

Captain Ilene decrees we'll stop at the nearest port to sell off the spices and cloth. We've got to keep turning a profit, after all. It never hurts to refresh our food stores either, but that's Maude's department, so I don't trouble myself too much over that. Old Maude's been at the job a long time. She won't let us starve.

Leo seems to have forgiven us. Or, at least, he's pointedly avoiding any mention of the events on the merchant vessel. He throws himself into the work. Scrubbing the deck still isn't an easy chore, but it appears to be easier than it once was for him, even with one injured arm. The work on-board the *Luck* has done him good. His muscles fill out his clothes pleasingly, and his skin is no longer peeling from exposure to the sun's rays. Instead, it's leant him a healthy pallor.

He looks up, feeling my eyes on him, and I swear...there is a moment where something disturbed flickers in their depths.

I'm squarely back in the box of being "just a pirate" again. Bloodthirsty. Criminal. An animal.

I salute him, wearing a quirk on my lips.

It's easier this way, after all.

But whether Leo has forgiven us or not, he quickly reminds me why he has failed to endear himself to the majority of the crew. Maybe he wants to continue avoiding me, but that part of him that is so desperate to find the Tigrid ship—the part of him that thirsts for answers—can't leave me alone. He finds me bent over my sword one day, sharpening it to a fine point.

He stands there a while, waiting for me to acknowledge him, the whisk of my stone against my blade the only sound between us as he waits in vain. Finally, he breaks first, his voice cracking the silence.

He clears his throat and coughs into his hand. "The rumor is we're making port," he says.

"You shouldn't believe everything you hear," I respond, not bothering to look up.

"Then we're *not* making port?"

"Well. You can believe *that* one, I suppose."

I set aside the whetstone and squint up at him. The sun casts his form into shadow, and I can't read his face. "Move just a titch to the left, would you?"

"Why?" The undercurrent of annoyance in his voice makes me want to sass him more, but I bite my tongue and hold fast to my patience.

"So I'm not blinking into the sunlight," I say. *You buffoon,* I don't add.

A quick shift and I can now see the expression on his face properly. A bit chastened, but a deep furrow in his brow that tells me he's got words to use and doesn't intend to mince them. Would that I could smooth out that furrow and remove it… I feel it would make a very handy gag.

"Is this stop related to the map?"

I *knew* that was the only reason he'd seek me out. He's barely spoken to me in days. I pick up the whetstone and give my blade an aggressive swipe. Of *course* it's about the bloody map.

"Isn't this a conversation better had with Captain Ilene?"

He frowns. "I'd love nothing more than to address my concerns with your captain. The problem is I can never find her."

I stow my sword, palm the whetstone, stand, and stretch. "Yeah, well...keep it up and you won't see hide nor hair of *me* either. The stop is related to profit. It keeps the crew happy. A happy crews do their work better."

He opens his mouth, but I cut him off before he gets the chance to speak.

"A happy crew, Mr. Wesson, finds your map *faster*."

He looks disgruntled, but nods, and shunts off, perhaps to find John. I watch him go, shaking my head. We'd come so close to an understanding between us, but that merchant ship and Celia had undone it all.

When we finally make port on Cavellia, it's less of an organized endeavor than our stop on Cielito was. This time, it's down to the Captain and me to fulfill our duties of selling off the spices and fabric we'd obtained from the merchant vessel. Most of the crew has already gone ashore for a bit of recreation when I go to her quarters and find her finishing up the laces on her boots.

"Ready, Gracie?" she asks, clapping her hands to her knees and rising.

I nod. "Aye." I raise the packet of spices and open my coat to show her the sample of silk I've tucked into my belt. Most times, we'd bring all of our cargo ashore, with the assistance of some of the other crew members, but in this case, Captain Ilene has a preferred buyer here on Cavellia. Samples will do for this particular shopper, so long as we have an accurate count of our stores. He'll take what he wants, and we'll have the crew transfer it to him. Money will change hands once the product is in his possession.

And not that Leo has any right to know, but I *do* plan to ask after the Tigrid ship here as well. This is one of the islands Jessamine mentioned, so I can kill two birds with a single stone. Thinking of it as the captain and I step off our longboat and onto the streets of Cavellia, I tug on the end of my braid. It's possible that on this trip, we could not only make ourselves a tidy profit, but also finally find the map.

And what will that mean for Leo? And John?

I blink hard, trying not to let my face reveal my emotions as I cast a side-long glance at the captain. It strikes me suddenly that I don't actually *know* what will become of the Wessons when we have the map in hand and Leo shows us how it's used. We'll no longer need them.

A twist of guilt, one that I've become halfway decent at suffocating of late, spirals through my gut.

With the way that little John's endeared himself to the crew and with the Captain Ilene's moral code being what it is, I don't *think* she would give the order for them to be killed. They can thank whatever deities they believe in that Celia isn't in charge there. But that doesn't mean Ilene won't throw them in the brig or abandon them on whichever island proves most convenient.

"Grace?"

I break from my reverie as the Captain raises a brow and motions through the doorway she's opened. I don't know how long she's been waiting for my attention, wrapped up in my thoughts as I've been.

"Any day now, Miss Porter," she says.

I clear my throat and walk into the small entryway. The hall is dark and lit with a single lantern, the heavy door an effective barrier against the day's light. Ilene leads the way forward into the shop, before she comes to a sudden halt, throwing a protective arm out to bar my path.

"Cap?" I cast her a quizzical look.

"Ahoy, ladies!" The raspy voice makes my blood curdle in my veins instantly. Whighorn starts forward from the sales counter, his men and Ilene's buyer looking up at us curiously.

The muscle in Captain Ilene's jaw works, a curl of hair near her ear twitching with the movement before she plasters a serene expression onto her face and drops the protective arm to let me hold my own. "Captain Whighorn," she says smoothly. "What a...pleasant surprise."

A surprise, it is. And I'm not certain Ilene knows that Whighorn and his crew were *also* on Cielito at the same time that we were. So she wouldn't know that this is akin to lightning striking the same place twice.

Once is a coincidence. Mere bad luck. But twice...twice is something else.

"Just have goods to trade, the same as you," he drawls. "We weren't near another port, and Bill's the best there is on Cavellia."

"That he is," she agrees. She tips her hat. "Well. We don't want to interrupt your bartering. My quartermaster and I will just step outside so that you can finish in peace."

"Kind of you," he says. "But we're on our way out. Have at him." His gaze flicks to me, and I suppress a shudder. "You're that captain's girl, aren't you?"

I stiffen at the mention of my father. "I'm *no one's.*"

"Sad. Not much to be said for a woman that no one bothers to claim." He swipes his arm under his nose, snorting as his two cohorts behind him chuckle lowly. "But that's a bit of a problem run rampant on that ship of yours, isn't it?"

I surge forward, backing him into the wall. My hand is on the hilt of my dagger in the blink of an eye. His rancid breath floats over my face as he laughs down at me, teeth glinting in the light.

"*Listen,* Whighorn—"

"Grace," Ilene warns lowly, and I bite my words back, feeling blood rise to the tip of my tongue from the force with which my teeth have clamped down on it. Reluctantly, I step away.

Whighorn slides free from the small space between our bodies and tilts his hat to me and then the Captain as he exits.

"Short leash you've got there," Whighorn's first lackey mutters to me, pointedly bumping into my shoulder on his way out.

"Bitch," the second one finishes, following his lead. I thunk into the wall of the narrow hallway and start after him as he leaves into the day's sunlight. I'm seeing black, my fist raised, intending to exact retribution, and then...

"*Grace.*" The captain's voice, much to my chagrin, is exactly as effective as a tether, snapping short as I reach its end. I jerk back, staring after the serpents in the dusty streets, and I slowly lower my fist.

They've gotten the last word, I suppose. For now.

Bill awaits us at his counter, polishing something with an old cloth. It's hard to tell if his efforts are having much of an effect on the object in this dim lighting, but a glimmer of light lands upon it and it casts its shine our way.

Bill looks up from his work as we approach, and his brows go up.

"Busy day," he comments. "Thought Whighorn and his lot would be all I'd get today."

Ilene is a master at this. A coy smile spreads across her cheeks. "Then I suppose it's your lucky day, isn't it, Billy boy?"

A reluctant smile tugs at one corner of his mouth. "Don't know about all *that*," he mutters. But he sets aside the silver teapot that he's been polishing and devotes his full attention to us. "What have you got for me?"

Hours later, we've finished our bartering with Bill, fetching a handsome price for the goods we've procured, and the Captain and I split to find more information about the Tigrid ship.

I'm also keeping a wary eye out for more of Whighorn and his goons…or Celia, for that matter. If I catch even a whiff of her fraternizing with them on Cavellia, the Captain will hear of it. And any worries of being called a snitch could go straight to hell.

But I see neither hide nor hair of either of them, and the well of leads on the Tigrid ship here has turned up dry.

I thank my third barkeep of the day for his time and head back to the *Luck*, where I find Ilene waiting. "Anything?" she asks, and at the shake of my head, she sighs. "Well, we turned a tidy profit. That'll keep the crew happy."

My eyes drift across the deck to Leo, who sits and stares at us as though he hopes to discern the content of our conversation by reading our lips...or maybe just by sheer force of will. I sigh, already dreading the conversation I know he hopes to have, and Ilene follows my gaze, barking out a laugh.

"Well," she says. "The crew will be happy. But we can't keep *everyone* happy." She claps a hand onto my shoulder and, since no one but Leo is on deck to see it, drops a kiss onto my forehead and smooths down the hairs along the crown of my head that have managed to escape from their braid. "Goodnight, Gracie."

"Night, Captain."

I hold Leo's gaze across the deck before I break our stare, shaking my head and heading for my quarters. I don't want to deal with him tonight. Just...not tonight.

Surprisingly, Leo doesn't pursue me that night or the next. I find his face in the crowd as I lean against the mizzenmast when Captain Ilene assembles the crew to make the announcement of our next stop. Little John stands in front of him, his big brother's hand on his shoulder. Leo's face is impassive as he stares up at me and Ilene.

It's Capri di Flores we're bound for next, Ilene says. It's the next best lead we have, the second island Jessamine mentioned. For all her claims that she'd been plying Whighorn and the serpents with drink in exchange for information, Celia hasn't offered up much of anything. And Capri di Flores makes sense. It's a popular port, where naval ships stop and get their last bits of fun in before sailing on home to resume their lives of obligation. With luck, that's what the Tigrid ship has chosen to do as well.

Capri doesn't pledge allegiance to any crown or government, so unlike some of the other ports we stop at, we've no need to anchor far from shore and row in. Here, we can find a dock, tie the *Lady Luck* up, and head off to explore the island.

We've found our spot, and a few of the crew have descended to the dock to tie us off. I'm securing my knots and giving them an experimental tug when I hear my name.

"Grace? Grace Porter, is that you?" I lift a hand to block the sunlight and squint up into the shadow of Old Man

Vail. His gray hair curls wet over the grizzle on his sun-weathered cheeks. He hitches up his belt over his portly belly as he scuffs his boot against the dock.

Anton Vail used to sail the Eleven Seas—he even had the start of a commanding presence out on the ocean before losing his leg in an accident. After that, he headed for shore.

"Couldn't find my sea legs after the sea decided to keep one of 'em," he's fond of joking. Now, he has himself a peg leg and its wood thumps against the dock as he steps forward, his weathered face breaking into a smile that lights his watery blue eyes and creases the wrinkles at their corners. "It *is* you. Your daddy was here just the other day, asking after you. Told him I hadn't seen your crew in too long, he sails off, and lo and behold, you turn up!" He shakes his head. "That tide... She works in mysterious ways, I'll tell you."

My gut twists. Mysterious ways indeed. If we'd been just a day or two earlier, I might have been forced to have the first meeting with my father that I'd had in...well, in *years*, I think, doing the math. After my mother and I left for Ilene and the *Luck*, we'd seen him only one more time.

I was too young then to have gotten the lay of the different islands dotting the seas we sailed, so I can't really say for certain which piece of land we'd found ourselves on.

I remembered eagerly pointing out the sails of his ship as we pulled into port, like clouds against the blue sky.

"Mama," I said, excited. I knew that silhouette. It was the naval vessel my parents always led me back to after we stopped to pay our respects to my father's liege and get his marching orders. "That's Papa's ship! Isn't it?"

Even at that age, and being well below their heights, I could feel the weight of the gaze that Ilene and my mother exchanged over my head.

"It does look like it," my mother said.

"Doesn't matter if it is," Ilene said, and she turned to spit bitterly into the sea.

I was right. It *was* my father's ship. And while Ilene attended to business, my mother and I found him in a bar, three sheets to the wind.

My mother had asked him for a legal divorce.

He had refused.

"You want the life of a criminal pirate? Fine. But I want you to know in the back of your mind that every dime you get will legally be mine." He glanced in my direction, over my mother's shoulder. I'd been just a step or two back, behind her petticoats. I remember the grip he had on her upper arm, the way her skin had pillowed around his fingers from the force of his grip on her. "That *everything* of yours is legally mine."

She'd stiffened and turned, following his gaze to me. And when she turned back to him, something in her face made him recoil. His hand dropped from her arm. The color drained from his face. He stumbled a step back and grasped backward for a bar stool to steady himself, unable to look away from her.

"Grace is mine," she hissed. "You do not touch her. Her name does not leave your mouth. You come anywhere near her and—"

He raised his shaking hands. "Understood. Yours."

She nodded, and whatever it was in her gaze that had so terrified him, it must have disappeared because he tucked his trembling hands back to his sides as the color slowly returned to his face. And he was finally able to break from her stare. When he turned his glance on me, there was something...something very like pity in his eyes.

He'd left the dark bar. Walked out into the sunlight. This time, I didn't try to cling to him. I didn't call out after him. I gripped my mother's navy blue skirt in my little hands as she brought a hand to rest on my head, stroking my hair. "Good riddance," she muttered below her breath.

I nodded, staring at the door he'd left through.

"It's you and me, Grace," my mother said. "You, me, and the sea. That's all we need."

My mother had no family. My father threw his away. And now, without either of them, it's just me.

Because the Mordgris...they'd stolen my mother away from. Pulled her into the sea she'd so loved. And they'd had the gall to wear her face while doing it.

But if I can find this map...they'll finally pay for all of that.

I snap back to the present, where old Anton is staring down at me, beginning to look a bit worried. "Grace? You all right?"

"Fine," I say, even as I know that I'm scowling. I tug at my knots to give myself something to do, and then it occurs to me that Anton Vail may be just the right person to ask about the Map of Omna's whereabouts. "Say, Anton...has a Tigrid ship come through here lately?"

He blinks, looking confused. "Well...yeah. Of course."

My hands are still on the ropes I'm securing, my heart skipping a beat. *Finally.* The Map of Omna is close at hand. The treasure of the Mordgris...and their destruction. It's all within reach.

"A Tigrid *naval* ship?" I ask, just to make certain. "Not just a bunch of Tigrid merchants."

Anton nods his head, looking a bit bewildered by my increasingly pointed questions.

"You're sure? When? How long ago?" I ask, hearing the eagerness in my voice.

Anton, bless him, quenches my thirst for information. "They cast off not more than a day or two ago," he says slowly, sounding puzzled.

A day. Two, at most. My heart picks up its pace, quickening with the excitement in my veins. If we figure out where they're going, we could catch them. The *Lady Luck*...she's fast. Faster than most naval vessels, by far. And they've only got a day or two's head start.

"You don't, by any chance, know where they were heading, do you?"

"Sure. They were heading on home now, weren't they?"

Without a word, I hurriedly begin to undo the knots I'd so meticulously tied securing the *Lady Luck* to the dock on Capri di Flores. My usually sure hands fumble and bump into each other in their haste, my breath catches in my throat.

"What are you—"

*There.* The ropes fall, the knots undone, and I leap up to my feet, tossing a quick "Thanks, Anton!" over my shoulder. I sprint back toward the ship, racing up the gangplank, where Sam is walking down.

"Grace? What are you—" I grab her shoulders, spin her about so she's walking back on-board and loop my arm through hers.

"Oh, Sammy girl." I grin and squeeze her arm. "The tides of our luck have just turned."

*From the ship's articles of the* Lady Luck*:*

*Each able body on-board the ship shall do her part in battle.*

I t seems like loosing the *Luck* from the dock takes an
eternity. I bounce anxiously on the balls of my feet as I
watch the girls toss the ropes back to the ship and
scramble back on-board.

In reality, it's been only moments, but we can't move
quickly enough. I chew on a hangnail between snapping
orders at the crew. Finally, our sails catch the wind, and
we're out on the open sea, flying a false Tigrid flag, in hot
pursuit of the naval ship.

The captain finds me in a still moment. "This could be
it, Gracie." She grins, and I find myself returning the smile.
Despite our disagreements over how to use the map, I love
sharing this moment with Ilene.

Her smile fades, and she scans my face. "It could all be
nothing," she warns. "I've been down this route before.

Thought I'd chase this map to the ends of the earth before I met your mother."

"And now?"

"Well." Her smile returns—weak, but it's there, even if its light doesn't quite reach her eyes. "Without your mother here, I have to say I quite like the idea of being a legend myself." She spreads her hand through the open air as if unfurling a scroll. "'Captain Ilene and the Map of Omna.'"

"Sounds like a tale you and Mama would have read to me when I was little," I say quietly.

It's a trick of the light, I'm sure, but for a moment, I think I see a tear glimmer in Ilene's eyes. "I bet you would have asked to hear it over and over again."

I let the wind whip past us, the crew rush around us, loathe to interrupt the nice moment we're having. But I can't just let it sit. Unbidden, it rises to my tongue. "Captain?" I start hesitantly. "About what we'll do with the map?"

She closes her eyes. "Grace," she says wearily. "*Please.*"

But the words won't be tamped down. "Just think of it," I urge her. "We'd—*you'd* be the stuff of myth twice over! We could find the map, destroy the Mordgris, secure their treasure, and—"

She cuts me a glare that silences me immediately. "Do you really believe that flattering my ego will convince me to endanger you and this *entire* crew so easily?" she asks with an eerie calm.

The cold, assessing look in her eyes is one that I have never been on the receiving end of, and I swallow, trying to decide how best to proceed.

"I just mean," I say slowly, "that I think it's an option worth presenting to the crew for voting. And I still intend to do so."

"You will do no. Such. Thing."

Now it's *my* glare that *she's* on the receiving end of, but she doesn't so much as flinch. "You don't get to decide that."

"As Captain—"

"As Captain, you can make decisions like whether or not we attack a ship," I say, my voice rising with my anger, not caring that I'm catching the attention of the crew. "As Captain, you decide if we should set a course for a respite on land. As *Captain,* you can be the deciding vote in a stalemate, but you *do not* get to take choices out of our hands. That is *not* what this ship is about. It is not why *any* of us are here."

I'd been so determined to discuss this calmly. Rationally. Like adults. But Ilene still sees me as a child.

Shaking my head, I move to shove past her, and she catches my arm. "I don't relish the idea of losing another member of my family, Grace."

"You're my captain, Ilene." I yank my arm free. "But you are *not* my mother."

She jerks back as if I've slapped her, and I stride away.

"It's real?" Leo finds me that evening with a careful hand on my forearm to grab my attention. We're well on our way by now, cruising smoothly along the best route from Capri di Flores to Tigri.

He grins, and I find myself struck by how the sun has reddened his cheeks in a strangely pleasing way. The smile makes his brown eyes dance. "You found the Tigrid rebels?"

I roll my eyes. The fact that he needs this confirmation from me when the rest of the crew hasn't shut up about what we're up to. Still, I can't resist their pull when my lips tug at my cheeks, my grin mirroring his. "Look around, Leo. We haven't found them quite yet. But I do consider this a promising lead."

"How promising?"

I pause, drawing out the moment for effect, reveling in the way he almost dances with anticipation. "I'd ready yourself for battle," I finally say when I think that he can take no more.

That grin again...it threatens to overtake his face. "Oh, you've no need to concern yourself with that, Grace. When it comes to the Tigrid rebels, I've been ready to fight for some time now. They have no honor. Spineless thieves. I intend to exact retribution for that on behalf of my king."

His hand slides down my arm, lingering at my wrist. His fingers hover over mine, and my heart jumps into my throat.

I yank my arm free.

"The retribution is yours. But remember...the map belongs to us," I remind him, busying myself with patting down my clothing and pretending to smooth away the sea salt that always coats my person. He takes a step away, coughing into his hand. Neither of us can meet the others' eyes. Heat rises into my cheeks as my heart slows to its normal beat.

"I could never forget it," Leo finally says, a respectful hush in his voice as he finds his nerve again and manages to meet my eyes once more.

Even now, with the excitement of an impending battle coursing through my veins, the heat of our connection fading, remorse fills its empty space. Leo had agreed to give us the map. To help us. As fixated as he is on the idea of honor, I can't imagine that the idea to double-cross us has so much as entered his mind. But obtaining the map and casting both him and his little brother off to the side once we have it has been our intention from the very beginning.

He'd hate us even more than the Tigrids if he knew. But he was right about us at the outset of this journey—I'm a pirate. We all are. We're ruthless. Unfeeling. Without remorse.

There's a certain cold comfort in knowing you were right about someone. I hope he can hold onto that.

It takes us but a day more along this route before our lookout alerts us that the Tigrid ship is within view of her spyglass, steady on the horizon. My breath catches in my throat when I hear her yell.

I'd expected—*hoped*—for as much. Anton hadn't seemed to think they were very far ahead of us. But the whims of the sea are flighty. It wouldn't be the first time they changed their mind, so I'd tried not to let my hopes get overly high.

The crew is busy about the deck as we pull closer, the Tigrid vessel coming into view without the aid of a spyglass. Squinting at the ship's shape, I cock my head to the side. There's something...familiar about it. Something that tugs at the edges of my memory. But I can't quite pull it into focus.

Our ship was built for speed, but the Tigrid ship is a sturdy thing, built for war. We pull closer and closer still, the wind whistling in my ears, and I stare at her. Have we encountered Tigrids before on an occasion that I've somehow forgotten about? My mind mentally flips through the catalog of battles we've fought and the treasures we've won, but still I come up empty.

It's only as we get closer, when I see how her sails rest against the backdrop of the sky—like little clouds—that the possibility occurs to me. I stiffen as Captain Ilene comes up next to me. I haven't quite forgiven her for our last exchange, but we're about to go into battle and she is still my captain. This isn't the time to let that resentment interfere with my work.

And that ship...it seems *so* familiar. I know plenty of pirate vessels. But there's only one naval ship that I have any degree of familiarity with.

"Captain...?" The curiosity—or is it trepidation? A grudging respect? I'm honestly not certain which emotion I feel—laces my voice.

"Ah," she sighs and curls her fingers over the railing. "I did wonder."

"Is it...is it *him*?"

She nods. It's a determined sort of movement. Decisive. "I do believe it is," she says.

A strangled sound escapes my throat, and she cuts me a sharp, sideways glance, scanning my face with concern. "The thought never occurred to you? You knew it was a Tigrid ship we were chasing all across the Eleven Seas."

I shake my head and blink hard to clear away the strange fog that's suddenly washed over my mind. "I guess I don't waste many thoughts on him. I've got more important things to do," I say, clearing my throat and swallowing the strange lump that's lodged itself there.

I forget, sometimes, that it was a Tigrid ship I'd spent the first years of my life living on.

And if Ilene and I both recognize it, the ship I'm staring at now is likely commanded by my father.

This, I suppose, explains why I've heard of his presence on the last island stops we've made over the past several weeks.

The ship we've been chasing all this time has been his.

It doesn't, however, explain the *other* part of the whispers surrounding him, that he's been asking after me and my mother. Why? Why *now*? Is it simple remorse? A general curiosity? Or something more?

I put it out of my mind for now. Clouded thoughts never made for favorable outcomes in battle. I need a clear head.

Mechanically, my hands move to the weapons secured on my belt, checking the position of my blade, familiarizing myself with the angle of my pistol's holster in case I need to yank it free.

*This* is what I can focus on. Leave my father as a meaningless figure, drifting on the sea. Blood or not, he's just the captain of another ship. That's all he's ever really been to me.

By the time we've pulled even with the ship, I'm ready. If any thoughts on the man at the helm of our opposing ship linger, they're indistinct shadows at the back of my mind. And the ones that remain revolve around how he will oppose us.

We must board the vessel quickly, or we'll risk falling prey to their cannons.

"What of *our* cannons, Captain?" Lila's question is a murmured one, but my ears pick it up nevertheless.

"Hold, for now," Ilene says almost absentmindedly from behind her spyglass, scanning the Tigrids' activity. She lowers it and stares hard across the water. "I've no need to destroy a fine ship. I'd hope their captain will return the sentiment."

Lila nods and turns to go, but Ilene catches her arm and looks at her seriously. "But, Lila. If their cannons fire upon us, consider permission granted for you to fire back."

"Aye, Captain." In a flash, she's gone again, off to supervise her gunners.

On the other side of the ship, half the crew has already disembarked and boarded the longboats, coming behind us at the stern. From the sea, once the rest of us have boarded, they'll climb the ropes we toss down to them to join the fray.

Judging by the lack of gunfire, my father's ship hasn't spotted our longboats...yet. All their attention is focused on those of us still on-board. But they're not blind. They'll spot the longboats soon, unless we provide them with an adequate distraction.

As for me, I stand on-board the *Luck's* deck, determined to be ready as I've ever been for a battle, despite the confusion in my heart. I don't know what will happen between myself and Ilene once we have the map. I don't know if I'll see my father in all the chaos. But I do know that my hand itches for a blade. For something I can take action upon.

Those of us on deck will brave the hail of bullets and charge into a tempest of steel, boarding their deck by pulling alongside them and flinging planks and ropes across. The aim here is speed, agility. We've got to land our planks on the least manned portions of their deck, and enough of us must rush across in order to defend it long enough for the remainder to board.

The first enemy shots are fired; the opening chords of combat struck.

The Tigrid shots come in warning at first, but the tempo quickly accelerates until the gunfire is in earnest. On the *Luck,* we duck below the rails of our ship, doing our best to obscure the Tigrids' sight lines. It's harder to fire at a warm body if you can't see it properly.

My blood joins the song, singing in my ear and beating a timpani in my heart as the anticipation grows.

When we land our planks, ducking beneath bullets, all other thoughts are gone; there is only the glorious symphony of battle awaiting me.

We stampede across the makeshift bridges. Already, the Mordgris swim below, but I force myself to ignore them. Even when I think I hear one of them use my mother's voice again.

*"For love and luck."*

But no one else seems to hear the whisper, and rather than confront the possibility that I've began to hear things, I thunder across a plank, over the raging tide. Even hearing my mother's favorite rallying cry doesn't shake my confidence. My toes are sure of my balance as I pull my sword free from its sheath, heart racing in fierce joy.

Ilene slices down the first bastard unfortunate enough to greet us. My steel fells the next one. Celia leaps onto the deck and into the fracas. And then, I lose track of all else. Men in uniform rush forward as we defend our position long enough to throw ropes overboard to the crew in the longboats, and they make haste up the side of the Tigrid ship to join us.

The naval officers simply cannot defend against our assault. Our numbers have them befuddled, wave after wave of women cresting over their rails. I take a chance, moving my eyes to glance overboard, and I grin. Our longboats are empty, but for the few women left behind to steer them back to the *Luck* when all of this is over.

A young member of the Tigrid crew tries to get the jump on me, but I seize him by the tail of his tied-back hair and wind it around my palm.

The boy's face is terrified beneath my hand as he cries out, wincing and ineffectually twisting to try and escape my grip. Below the ecstasy of battle, I feel a pang of sympathy for him. He can't be older than thirteen years old. He'd likely been pressed into service or had no other choice but to join up and earn a wage to send home.

He doesn't want to die here. And I don't wish to serve as his executioner.

"Don't be a fool, boy," I say. "Is this your first battle?"

He swallows hard. "No, miss."

"Second?"

He nods furiously. "But last one, I was just a powder monkey at the guns. The Allarians didn't come aboard."

A yell rises above the rest of the battle—a war cry. An answering gunshot echoes as the shout turns to a strangled sound, cutting its owner's fight short. The boy's eyes grow wide.

"Tell me what I wish to know," I say, bending close to his face, "and I'll let you go. You can find a safe space to hide. No one will ever know."

He looks to the floor, unable to meet my gaze. His voice is soft, and I find that I have to strain to hear him when he whispers, "I'll be executed for cowardice, miss."

"Look around," I say, growing impatient. He yelps as I twist his hair harder and force his attention in the direction of the battle. "You rushed in with the rest of them, and they're quite busy. No one is going to notice your absence. *Talk* to me and you will live to see another day. Now. When you fought the Allarians, your crew took a map from them. I have a need of that map."

This is the understatement of the century. I don't just need the map. I'm *desperate* for it. My blood is hot with anticipation, with the idea that it is within my grasp. That the *Mordgris* are within my grasp.

That my mother might be, too.

The boy's eyes flicker in recognition and move fruitlessly across the deck, looking for a comrade-in-arms to save him. I know this boy's ilk. He's like Leo. He believes in honor. To tell me what I want to know is, to him, an unthinkable betrayal of his crew and country.

But fortunately for me, his will to live outweighs that inconvenient sense of morality.

"It's in the captain's quarters," he blurts. "Across the deck, down the stairs, through the doors that meet you at the stairs' end."

I release him, and he takes a moment to look down at the sword in his hand and back up at me as though gauging his chance. I lift my own in warning.

"I was kind once, boy," I say quietly. "I won't be so sweet to you again."

With that warning, he takes the gift he's been given and bolts away, disappearing between Celia and Ann, in the throes of battle.

Somehow, Leo manages to break from the fracas when he sees my purposeful stride, the way I fling would-be opponents away from me as easily as if swatting at flies.

"Have you found it?" he pants as he reaches me. His face is red with effort, and sweat streams down his cheeks. One of the Tigrids charges him, but he neatly steps aside. When the man turns again and runs at me, I quickly glean that he's not one of their better duelers. It takes all of one...two...*three* clashes before I jab into an opening, striking true, the threat dispelled.

"Not yet." I turn, grinning, hearing the thump as the body falls behind me, my steel practically singing in my hand. I look up with a fierce smile to meet Leo's gaze.

But he doesn't return it. Instead, he takes an alarmed step backward when our eyes collide.

I check behind me, expecting to see an approaching attacker. The deck is still occupied with battle and blood, but no one rushes toward us. They're too preoccupied with the rest of the crew. My grin fades as I turn back to Leo. "What? What is it?"

"It was... Your eyes..." He trails off and swallows, steps closer and scrutinizes my face. I stare back up at him, perplexed. "Nothing," he says finally, shaking his head. "Must have been a trick of the light."

Celia is right above us now, near the helm. The clang of steel is missing from up above. She's either just searching for the map or has simply already dispatched her foes.

"Anything, Miss Munn?" I holler to be heard over all else.

Her movement overhead stills. "No, Miss Porter. Not yet. You?"

I don't answer her as, instead, I take Leo's hand. "Come on," I say. My feet dance nimbly between battling bodies, and I lead him belowdecks, where the boy said the captain's cabin was.

I could have found my own way here, even without the directions. Once I was told the location of the map, that was it. I wish that the map itself was pulling me to it, some sort of mythical connection, but it's like...muscle memory.

I *remember* this ship.

I remember the feel of its planks beneath my feet. When I look down at my boots clipping across its weathered wood, I have to blink back the vision of much smaller feet, laced into soft blue slippers, covering the same surface. Below the screams and clashing steel is my high-pitched giggle as my mother chased me over the deck.

"Let's go find that map of yours," I tell Leo, raising my voice to drown out the sound of my past.

"No," he says, giving my hand a squeeze and quickening his steps to keep pace with me. "When we find it, it's *your* map." His lips quirk up. "At least, until we find you a suitable treasure."

We come to a screeching halt before the doors of the captain's quarters.

There are no shadows from my memory here. There hardly needs to be. The pockmarked doors are just the same, perhaps with a few more nicks. I couldn't reach the round, iron handles as a child, but there is no straining to reach them now. My father may be behind these doors. But so, too, could the map.

My hands hover over the metal, and without quite meaning them to, my eyes flicker to Leo's.

"Go on, then," he urges, not understanding my hesitation. "But be on your guard."

I release Leo to take the iron in hand and give it an experimental push. Not even locked. How arrogant can you be? With that test concluded, I give the door a mighty shove and Leo and I move inside.

The first things my eyes fixate in the dim chamber on are the dark, twin barrels of a pistol aimed directly at our heads.

My sword is out in an instant, pointed toward the enemy weapon.

The door clicks shut behind us, sealing us in with the gun and its owner. The blocked exit muffles the noises of battle on the deck above so that we can hear a second, louder click—the sound of the pistol being cocked. My gaze travels past the black metal, past its clip, to the hand clutching it, and then to the hand's mate, resting atop an old, wrinkled sheet of paper. My heart takes refuge in my throat at the sight.

It is, without a doubt, the map we've been seeking for months now. It has to be. Lazy spirals are drawn and then erased by an invisible artist, the inkwork appearing and then vanishing all over its surface. It's magicked. And I know of no other reason a magical document would be here unless it is the Map of Omna and Leo had told us the truth.

Finally, I am able to tear my eyes from the parchment to look into my father's eyes for the first time in years.

"I thought—" His voice sounds different. I remember a sturdy, confident sound, but there's a waver in it now and a rasp, like a snake's rattle. "I thought, when I saw the ship, when I saw a bunch of bitches clamber their way onto my decks. I thought it might be you."

The insults are precisely what I would have expected from him. They have no effect on me. My hand holds my sword steady in the air before me, but the muscles in my arms are burning from its weight. My eyes also burn as I stare at my father, refusing to blink. I nearly manage to forget Leo, my field of vision narrowing to the Captain and his gun.

"I'd hoped it would be that bitch Ilene who came for the map, but—wait. Where is your mother?" he asks suddenly, interrupting his own stream of thought.

This *does* have an effect on me. My blade wavers at the unexpected mention of Mama. "What, in all of the Eleven Seas, makes you think that you have *any* right to speak of her? Why would you *care* if she was here?" I ask, my voice low.

"I care if she's on my ship," he says. "She's the worst of all of them." Without taking his gaze from mine, he spits in disdain.

Rage grips me. My teeth feel sharper. I could tear his flesh from his bones. I'll teach him to speak ill of my mother if I have to rend him in two. I step forward, but he lifts his gun higher in warning.

From the corner of my eye, I see Leo look from my father, to me, and back again. "Grace?" he says. "Do you know this man?"

"Don't worry," I say, without taking my eyes off my father. "He's nothing. I'll handle it."

The captain's gaze slides to Leo as he continues speaking to me through clenched teeth. "You know, I imagined a lot of things when I thought of you over the years. I hoped that you'd given up this life. Returned to the ways of proper society. But even if that was too much to hope for, I *never* could have dreamed up some sort of nightmare of a story in which you teamed up with Allarian *filth*."

Leo's sword raises alongside mine, chest puffed up like an indignant peacock.

"At least *Allarians* know the definitions of honor and loyalty. You Tigrids must have forgotten what they mean," he seethes, starting for my father.

I stop him with a foot stuck out to the side and cut him a warning glance. "Don't," I say lowly. Leo stops in his tracks, and I look back to my father.

"You've been asking after me and Mama," I say, and something shifts in his eyes.

"I haven't the faintest idea what you could be talking about," he says shortly.

"No?" I ask, bitterness coating my words. "Jessamine on Cielito sings a different tune. And Anton Vail on Capri di Flores tells another tale. So does Bill on Cavellia. If you could sail as quickly as you can apparently flap your gums, we may never have caught up to your ship."

His lip curls in distaste. "You're as insolent as your mother."

I take a step forward and he has an answering lift of his gun once more, but this time I notice a tremor in his hand and I raise a brow at the sight of it.

I take another step. And another, ignoring the warnings of both my father and Leo who tell me "don't" and "stop"; "what are you *doing*?" and "I'm warning you."

When another step brings the tip of my blade level with his heart and still he hasn't pulled the trigger, I find that my hand is trembling on the hilt, an echo of his.

"You don't actually want to shoot me," I realize, understanding dawning. "Do you?"

He doesn't utter a word, though his eyes narrow in a glare.

"Getting soft in your advancing age, old man?"

"Grace," Leo tries again, keeping his suspicious gaze on my father and leaning closer to me so that he's speaking lowly into my ear. "I want the map, too, but—"

"He's my father," I say, finally looking away from him in time to see Leo's eyes widen with shock. "And he's not going to shoot me. Are you?" I ask, looking back to the old captain.

A muscle in his jaw works. His teeth grind together, and finally he grits out a "no" as if it physically pains him.

His gun settles onto the desk, conceding defeat.

I stow my cutlass and sweep the map from under his careless palm. "Good. I'll be taking this, then."

"Hold." His pistol comes up again and, this time, comes to rest on Leo. "I said I wouldn't shoot *you*. But far as I'm concerned, the world would be a better place with one less piece of Allarian trash taking up space on it."

Without thinking twice, I step in front of the gun.

"*Move*," my father growls.

But the days when I obeyed him are long since passed. My heart pounds as I stare down his steely gaze. If I can make an effective shield for Leo, I'll do it.

I only hope my father meant it when he said he wouldn't shoot me.

Blood thrashing in my ears, I all but miss the sound of the door creaking open. I don't process the sound until I feel the cool kiss steel upon my neck. A blade. My hair is tugged backward into a male body.

*Not someone from the* Luck *providing us with some support, then*, I think grimly.

"Hello there, lass," the man breathes as my father jumps to his feet, chair clattering to the ground as he knocks it over in his haste. "I see you've found yourself something that doesn't belong to you. Kindly return the map to the captain there and—"

He's not given the chance to finish his sentence as Leo lunges toward my hip, pulls my pistol from the holster where it's resting so peacefully, takes aim, and fires.

The gunshot rings in my ears as the man and his arm drop to the floor like a heavy anchor in the sea.

My ears are still ringing as Leo turns to me and grins, and I can just make out his words, as if he's speaking them underwater, from a great distance.

"I told you that I was an excellent shot."

*From the ship's articles of the* Lady Luck:

*Extra rations shall be distributed only at the discretion of the captain.*

9

A roar of celebration greets us when Leo and I return above deck, and I brandish the rolled-up map above my head like a baton. We'd seized the opportunity belowdecks to tie my father's wrists to his desk. He'll get free eventually, but for now, he won't pose any further complications.

The battle is still in progress, but it's clear the odds are in the *Luck's* favor. Bodies dot the deck. Unconscious or dead, I don't know, but there are far more male than female forms lying about.

Ann grunts as she and her opponent fall back against the rail, their blades locked against their chests. A bead of sweat falls down Ann's red face as she breaks away, then charges her opponent, going for his legs. The man wasn't expecting that; she gets his legs higher than her shoulder before it seems to occur to him what she's doing. His sword clatters to the deck as he grabs desperately for a grip on the railing. He manages to get one. But Ann succeeds in hoisting his body over the side of the ship, where he dangles like a worm for bait.

My eyes travel to the waves below, to the school of Mordgris that Ann is about to feed. They wear no one's faces but their own now, just a blank canvas of gray stretched over a skull. No eyes. No nose. Just rows and rows of needle teeth, stretched in a horrifying grin.

Ann swallows, seeing them, but her disconcert at the sight isn't enough to dissuade her from disposing of this opponent. This man won't sate their hunger. He's just enough to whet their appetites.

She pries his fingers loose from the rail, and the man drops, plummeting to the waves below. I nearly turn into Leo to hide my eyes, my stomach lurching in horror, but I make myself watch.

The Mordgris are on the man in an instant, arching toward him with a grace dolphins usually reserve for leaping through the waves. Tens of hands are on the man, holding him on the surface while their teeth tear gashes into his neck. Before long, the ocean is stained red, and the man's body is unrecognizable as human. Just a fillet of meat.

Did this happen to Mama, too?

This soon after meeting with my father, she's close to the forefront of my thoughts. If they did this to my mother, the Mordgris dragged her away first. I'd *watched* them pull her away. But they're not creatures of restraint, the Mordgris. I don't see them biding their time to play with their prey.

They'd all grabbed her certainly. She hadn't been able to escape as they'd pulled her below the surface, each of them taunting us by donning her face. But there hadn't been a sea of blood staining the waters red. No bits of flesh floating across the waves.

She couldn't have survived under the water. I know that. But the fact that they didn't kill her outright makes hope leap in my chest.

It's all of that that makes me cling to the slim possibility that my mother might still be alive.

I do my best to banish the thought, trying to make logic take hold. But the doubt—the *hope*—persists stubbornly. It isn't something I can waste time thinking about, however. The battle winds to a close.

"Did you see him?" Captain Ilene finds me, her eyes scanning the deck. She watches Bonnie in a detached manner as Bonnie kicks at a sailor struggling to his feet.

"Stay down," Bonnie tells him. "The day is lost. Your life need not be."

I pretend not to know of whom she speaks. "See who, Captain?"

"Grace."

"Yes, I saw him." I drop the pretense. "But it doesn't matter. He lives and will go on with his life, as will I." I brandish the map at her with a grin. "Though *one* of us will be considerably richer than the other."

She grins. "Good work, Gracie. Back to the ship?"

"Back to the ship."

It's not a clean break as we make for the *Luck*. The Tigrid sailors are determined to retrieve their hard-won prize, believing it would secure them a victory over the Allarian king. And maybe it would have, had they been our equals in warfare. But that isn't the case as our crew beats a hasty retreat, sending the few who manage to follow us back on-board the *Luck's* deck spilling to the water and to the Mordgris below.

I ignore the way my stomach lurches, feeding the Mordgris yet another meal. I don't want to provide them sustenance. I fear it will only make them stronger.

"Forget climbing onto the longboats. They've returned. We'll go over the planks," Ilene orders. She stands at one of the temporary bridges connecting our ships, wheeling her arm toward the *Luck* to direct the crew home. The women manning the longboats have already rowed toward our ship, making the wise decision to steer clear of the dangerous Mordgris.

Once the majority of our crew has safely returned to the *Lady Luck,* Captain Ilene gives the order to hoist the anchor, let fly our colors, and loose our sails.

I watch one unmistakable figure at the railing of the Tigrid ship. My father's managed to free himself. His expression is impassive, so I make mine match as we lock eyes.

It feels as though we all hold our breath as we sail away. By the time the Tigrid manage to cobble their wits back together and ready their cannons to fire at us, we're well out of their range, the cannonballs splashing uselessly into the water in our wake. They give chase for a while, but with a heavy warship like theirs, they haven't got a prayer of catching up with us.

It's just us and the sky on the horizon. No one else.

Finally, Celia cocks her hip confidently and loudly asks, "Shall I fetch the brandy then, Captain?"

A huge cheer goes up from the crew when Captain Ilene responds, "We just got the *Map of Omna.* I want more than just brandy up here. Everyone gets her choice of drink. Tonight, we drink like queens!"

Celia disappears, bringing her favorite brandy back with her when she returns from where she she'd hidden it in the gullery. The barrels of rum are fetched, along with bottles of whiskey and brandy. A carafe of wine—the fancy stuff—pulled from the captain's very own stores. There are lanterns, lit carefully away from the guns. And before long, the sun has set into a sea cast glowing red.

When the sky darkens, the stars and moon are bright. One of the ladies pulls out her fiddle, another fishes out her flute, and some start to dance about in their merriment. John listens, rapt, to Maude's account of the battle. His expression is awed, taking in every detail as she gestures dramatically, detailing the thrilling tale.

As for me, I'm happy watching the festivities, perched upon one of the large crates someone has pulled to the center of the deck. A warm body joins me.

"Do you mind the company?" Leo asks.

I grin, tossing him a wink so he knows I'm joking when I say, "I think I can stand the company of a spoiled nobleman. That is, if *you're* not terrified to be in such close proximity to a pirate."

His eyes, warm with an emotion that sets a fire to light in me, rove my body. "I think I'll manage somehow."

He settles in beside me on the barrel, taking care at first not to nudge my leg with his. I suppose he thinks it would be ungentlemanly of him to presume.

He may be a gentleman...but lucky for him, I'm no lady.

I slide the inch or so that lays between us to let my leg fall against his. I can feel the warmth of his skin through my breeches. Clammy, too, with the night air. My bare ankle rubs his.

His gaze flits down to his skin against mine, and he swallows, looking nervous, before he's able to look up at me once again.

"What do you think?" I ask, purposely making the question suggestive; my voice, sultry.

Alarmed, his eyes shoot wide, and I laugh, finally moving my leg away so he can relax. The tension leaves his body immediately.

I *almost* feel bad for toying with the poor lad this way…but not quite.

"What do you think of this life we lead?" I ask. I gesture to the ship at large. The sails look beautiful against the night's blanket of starry skies. Magical, even. Like something out of a storybook. Even the crew looks like they could have marched out of someone's tall tale. Sam's hair is flying loose from beneath her bandanna as she twirls around, arm in arm with Bonnie. Bonnie's braids whip around her face, and she throws her face to the sky, laughing in the light of the moon.

Captain Ilene watches us all with amused eyes.

Celia takes over the flute-playing and plays a merry tune, eyes glittering, and my thoughts transfer from Leo to her. Celia had been less…bloodthirsty in this battle. But I'd seen her everywhere, it seemed, aboard the Tigrid ship.

She was just looking for the map. That's what we were *all* doing on the ship.

Still…something in me whispers that it's more.

But I have no proof of it. Nothing more than the fact that I don't trust her. I haven't since I was a child. Is that simply because it's always down to the two of us for the title of quartermaster and first mate? Perhaps. Who's to say that in her shoes, *she* wouldn't be equally suspicious of *me*? She may even think I'm colluding with the Wesson boys.

I don't know who I think *she's* colluding with.

Her eyes meet mine, and her lips quirk up over her flute, disrupting her song.

Maybe my perception of her is only coloring my judgement.

Maybe.

But she has been sending an awful lot of letters lately.

"I think…" Leo's voice brings me back to him, reminding me that I'd asked him a question. "I think that this life is strange. But sometimes wonderful, in its own way."

"That way wouldn't happen to be the freedom we've got, would it?"

"It's…" He trails off, searching for words. "It's a lot of things. The freedom, yes, but also, there's the sense of camaraderie among you, the sea air, the sun, the wind in your face—"

"The rum," I interrupt with a grin, and he laughs, shaking his head.

"Oh, certainly." He laughs, rolling his eyes and holding his drink up, affecting a lofty tone. "The *fine* vintage of piss-poor, watered-down rum you drink would be enough on its own to send one scrambling to join your ranks."

I put a hand to my heart, blinking dramatically, as if shocked and appalled. "Why, milord." I fan myself. "Such foul language."

"Avast, me hearty," he says with a wink, and I can't help the burst of laughter that flies out of me. From a true and crude pirate, the likes of Whighorn, a phrase like that would go perfectly well with the leer that was bound to accompany it. But from Lord Leonardo Wesson, delivered in his posh and noble accent, every vowel and consonant carefully enunciated, it's nothing short of ridiculous.

He waits until my laughter dies down and grins sheepishly. "Too much?"

"Far, far too much," I say, still catching my breath from laughing. And yet...it's also just the right amount.

Sam catches my eye and winks. I return it.

"And the battle," I say. "What did you think of that?"

"That..." His words vanish into the ether once again, and he shakes his head. "That was..."

There's something in his eyes as his thoughts drift back to today's battle. The Tigrid battle had been different from the merchant vessel we'd taken. Less violence. Less of a thirst for blood and more a thrill of the hunt. I'd seen something in his eyes during both battles, before the first had taken a turn for the worse. That same something, a small glimmer, a little thrill, lights them once again as he reminisces about today, and it makes me nudge his knee and say—

"It suits you, you know."

He stiffens, a knot tightened. "I beg your pardon?"

"This life. You were strange, when you came on-board the *Luck*. This life was new to you, but you've acclimated well. You've taken to it like…well, like a fish to water." I laugh over the feeble joke.

The warmth of his leg next to mine vanishes, and Leo stands up from the crate, looking down at me with a stony expression. "Generally, madam, when one begs one's pardon, they are giving you a chance to take your words back."

*Madam?*

"Take it back?" I'm genuinely bewildered for a moment before irritation rises. "If you had paid attention for one moment, *Lord Wesson*—" The stormy expression pinches together as he winces, but it's quickly back in place, clouds moving in over his eyebrows. "—you may have cottoned on to the fact that I don't *take* my words back. *Or* my actions.

157

You *might,* in fact, recall that it is that *precise* characteristic that you and your brother have to thank for *your life."*

My ire is quick to rise to meet his insult, and the adrenaline of it sends me shaking. He looks taken aback, considering my words, knowing—he *has* to know—that it's true. I'd saved him and John from the Mordgris, defying the captain's orders, defying the rules of the *Lady Luck.* If I hadn't stood by that decision, Anne, Celia, and the rest of them would have felt no guilt about throwing them overboard for the Mordgris to have as their dessert.

"You already know how grateful I am—" he starts, and I clamber to my feet, my body rising to meet him.

"I *don't* actually. All you've done since you got on-board is act *entitled.* Entitled to meet with my captain despite the fact that she has a *ship* to run. Entitled to information that you've no right to. Entitled to have input on the ship's course, our rations, our stops. *Actual* members of our crew act less entitled than you, Wesson."

"I told you not to call—"

"I am the *quartermaster of this ship!*" I bellow. "I will call you whatever I damn well please."

My chest is heaving, and he stares at me as if he has never seen me before.

Slowly, haltingly—as if he is a hinge in need of oiling—he bends, delivering me a mocking bow. "Well... *quartermaster...*I thank you for your intended compliment."

He spits the word so that I know it for the insult it is. "But I think you're far more suited to the life of a filthy pirate than I."

He turns and storms away, pausing only briefly to collect John before they leave me standing among the still crew, firelight flickering in the barrel beside me.

It's only then that I realize the music has stopped.

I spend a little more time on deck, celebrating with my crew.

*And why not?* I think, surly as I take another drink. It's a major victory for us. The map is in hand, which means riches are all but assured.

I let my annoyance and anger with Leo fade into the background, in favor of the hope that throbs inside of me as if it has its own heartbeat. The crew and I can find the Mordgris. We can destroy them.

The only obstacle left is to convince them that it's worth it.

I join in the dancing, twining my arm through Sam's. She bestows a big sloppy kiss on my cheek.

"I can do it, Grace," she says. Her breath is ripe with the scent of alcohol. We switch arms and turn around the lanterns again. "Once we use the map to find a treasure, I can get my own ship now. Be master of my own fate."

This makes me lurch to a stop. The rub of it is, I don't *want* Sam to leave.

"You...*could*," I say carefully. "But, Sam, why would you want to leave us? We're your family."

Her glassy eyes crinkle, and she tugs at one of my curls. "*You're* my family. But the rest... Things aren't as peaceful on-board as they once were."

"What does that mean?"

Her eyes drift over to Celia, who has set aside her flute in favor of watching us as the fiddler plays on. "Pay attention, Gracie."

"To Celia?"

"To Celia, yes. But...she's not alone." She stretches her arms over her head and stifles a yawn. "I've got to head to my bunk. The ship is starting to pitch in a way that I don't think is due to the waves." She winks. "See you topside in the morning, Miss Porter."

I watch her go and let my eyes drift over the women still on the deck, wondering who is celebrating our ship's victory and who might be celebrating plans of their own.

And suddenly, I feel rather tired myself. I think I'll go to bed, too.

It takes a bit of time, but I finally drop off to sleep, only to be awakened by a knock at my door. A quick internal survey tells me I haven't been asleep long...just long enough to have a bit of time unaccounted for.

I stretch and step from the bed. I suspect that it's Captain Ilene. It's unusual for her to come for a chat this late at night, but not altogether unheard of. The dead of night is a good time to have a discussion, with little chance that we'll be overheard by another member of the crew. We didn't speak at the celebration, and while I don't relish the thought of arguing again over potential destinations, it isn't a topic that's going to go away.

But when I swing open my door, it's not the captain waiting there. It's Leo, arm braced against the doorframe, hair falling over his brow. He lifts sorrow-filled brown eyes to mine, and I start, blinking.

"Leo, I'm—" I start and then slam down on the urge to apologize. "If you're here expecting an apology, you're about to be sorely disappoint—"

Leo places a single finger onto my lips. "Shh," he says. "That's not why I'm here." He pauses, eyes scanning the room behind me. "May I come in?"

I step aside, letting him enter and the door close behind him. "I suppose."

He turns a slow circle in my room, taking in the surroundings, before turning to face me once again. My eyes search his. He'd been so angry. Why the change of heart? "Why *are* you here?"

His hand lifts, hesitates, then rests against my cheek, where his thumb strokes slowly. His mouth lowers to my ear. "*Why do you think?*"

I hesitate myself...but only for an instant.

Then, I give in. I melt into his touch. What harm could it do, really? He was angry. So was I. Best we work that out rather than internalize all of it.

I am used to touching. Paid or unpaid, there have been many a port of call in the past several years and many a touch. A lover's hand on my body isn't unfamiliar, but in the past, it's been hard. Fast. A means to an end; pleasurable...but fleeting.

This... My breath hitches as his hand skims my body, comes to rest on my abdomen. His own breath grows ragged, and his lips dip to my neck. I wouldn't mind if *this* lasted.

Both of his hands rest against my hips so that his are flush against mine. Eyes steady on my face, as though gauging any uncertainty I may feel, he backs me the few paces across my small cabin that it takes to reach my bed. When the backs of my knees hit the bed, I lean back and he comes with me.

Then, finally, his lips are on mine. It's not the sort of kiss that I would have expected from Leo. It's domineering, confident, assertive. His tongue sweeps inside as though plundering my mouth.

I pull back to release a shaky breath, and he raises a brow. "If you tell *any* of the crew..." I warn.

He reclaims my lips, snatching them with his, teeth scraping my bottom lip. "It's our secret," he assures me.

With impatient hands, he tugs my hair loose from its ribbon and it goes spilling over my shoulders. "Such pretty curls," he says. His hands dive into my tresses as he speaks into my neck. "Like waves. Like your mother's."

I stiffen in his arms, growing rigid with horror. My eyes, only a moment before closed and floating on a sea of sensation, shoot wide open. The voice near my throat didn't belong to Leo, but it's as familiar to me as my own.

Teeth—far too many, far too *sharp,* I now realize, to belong to a human mouth—scrape my neck.

"*Stay off the island, sweetling,*" my mother's voice hisses.

Driven on pure instinct, I shove at the shoulders that still bear Leo's shape, kick out at his thighs. I am sent slamming against the wall behind my bed, clutching at my neck in horror.

The rush of adrenaline leaves me breathless, panting, as the creature in my bed cackles and slowly crawls up toward me like it's climbing a wall. Its long black nails are like iron. Its face oscillates between the familiar visage of my mother's face, Leo's, and the grotesque, all-too-familiar vision of the Mordgris. Its bones—gods, does it *have* bones?—dissolve into a thick black smoke, and almost immediately reform once more into what look like very *solid* hands, reaching for me.

"Get out," I croak, pressing into the wall, trying to gain even an inch more of distance between myself and the Mordgris.

And, miraculously, the hands that are only inches from my throat freeze.

I blink hard, for a moment thinking that I'd imagined it. But no…the creature has definitely paused, head angled to the side as if in confusion.

"You—" It pauses, and in the space of a blink, it *warps*, cycling through discarded appearances so quickly that I can't make out individual features. It settles on Leo, and it's more unsettling than before, his face with the mismatched claws and squid-ink form. "You invited me in," it says, in Leo's smooth tenor.

"I invited *Leo* in," I correct, my voice stronger. Steadier. Gods, can the Mordgris actually be reasoned with? "You are not welcome here. Leave."

Again, Leo's features disappear, giving way to the Mordgris, indistinguishable from its brethren.

"And *you* are not welcome on the island," it whispers. Before, finally, at *last*, its form collapses into black vapor and disappears through cracks between the planks of a ship, the pounding of my heart and the scratches on my neck the only signs it was ever here at all.

*From the ship's articles of the* Lady Luck:

*Crew shall not steal from crew.*

I put a trembling hand to my lips as the Mordgris melts away through cracks in the ship, an inky black smoke disappearing through the wall.

I've never seen a Mordgris shed their form to assume the entire body of a human like that. I've never seen one of them leave the water before. I didn't know that they *could*.

I collapse onto my bunk, the bedding still mussed from where I'd fallen backward, entangled in Leo's—in the *Mordgris's, gods*—arms. I feel... I'm—I don't know how to define it. It had *touched* me. Its dark nails had scraped against my skin, its hundreds of needle teeth had nibbled at my neck, it—

I shudder violently, fumbling blindly for my flask and the steadiness that the whiskey will bring me. I need the burn to ground me.

The wave of relief when my hands close around the cool metal feels so palpable, I'm surprised the room hasn't flooded.

I settle back against the wall, staring at the spot where the last bit of Mordgris vapor vanished, feeling steadier as I sip the drink, lost in thought.

Once I get past the initial horror of the incident, I force myself to review what I've learned. Before this, I'd known that the Mordgris could steal faces and the voices that match. But I *hadn't* known they could transform completely. I *hadn't* known they could board a ship. I *hadn't* known they could erupt into a dark vapor and simply vanish.

Indeed, the Mordgris had given me a lot to think about.

And what had it said, just before it'd vanished? I think back to the hot breath, the whisper hissed against my ear.

*"Stay off the island, sweetling."*

I sit bolt upright. The island.

They know we have the map.

I pace my chambers, my flask safely tucked away, my thoughts racing. Somehow, because of whatever reason they follow me, we'd led the Mordgris straight to the map that could assure their destruction. What if they took it? What if they destroyed *it* before we had a chance to destroy *them?*

The Mordgris had found its way into my room, bold as you please. What was to stop them from doing the same thing to Captain Ilene? Why wouldn't they just drift into her quarters, slipping between the cracks, and take the map for their own? Maybe they had already done it.

But what if they hadn't already done it?

The Mordgris had shown me a bit of their hand with this move. Not much—a single card, if that. But the fact that we've found the map...it worries them. And *that* means something to me. It means I have a hope. I hope of *finding* their damn island and destroying it, burning it to ashes if I have to. All the legends say that the Mordgris' power is tied to their treasure. Take that from them and they will follow.

The crew would object, I know. But I allow myself to dream of not just stealing it from the Mordgris, but setting it aflame. And then I'll scatter its ashes across the open sea so that I can sail boldly across their grave.

But all of that depends on the map.

I have to know if the map is still ours. I have to. I can't just sit here and wait to find out. I need to know if the map is safe. If the hunt and battle have all been for naught.

When I leave my chambers, the full moon lights my path across the deck. Its light is plenty to see by, and I'm grateful, for I dare not carry a torch. There are still a few lanterns lit, a few stragglers celebrating on the far side of the deck. Some of them have fallen asleep right where they sit. Others stare forward as if spellbound, wavering every so often. Too much to drink.

I should not be creeping into Captain Ilene's quarters in the dead of night. I know this. I know this, and yet I'm doing it anyway, attempting to stay out of sight of the crow's nest and remaining revelers. If they see me topside, it's fine. The trouble will be if they see me cracking Ilene's door open. If they see me slip inside to examine the top of her desk.

And if they see me using my lock picks on her desk drawer, well...then I've stepped about knee-high in deep shit.

*I'm doing this for the good of the crew,* I tell myself, using my key to unlock Ilene's quarters. I sidle between the frame and the door that I've coaxed open. The moon's light leaks into the opening before I quickly shut it behind me.

Once my eyes adjust, they fall on her desk. My picks click quietly on the lock of the captain's desk. *Shhhh,* I think desperately, keeping one eye to the door that separates Captain Ilene's work quarters from her sleep quarters. It isn't loud, but the captain is a light sleeper.

The lock clicks into place, and I fight the urge to yell in victory. Instead, as slowly as possible, so as not to create any extra noise, I slide the drawer out and lift the false bottom.

Immediately, my shoulders sag in relief, seeing the rolled-up, ancient piece of parchment. The paper is yellowed with age, but secure. Those same lazy spirals I'd seen earlier roll over the parchment, as easily as waves on a sea.

The map is here. Everything is as it should be.

My hands move to the edge of the drawer, intending to push it closed, but something stops me. The map is safe, but for how much longer? What if the Mordgris find it?

This map is the key to everything: to the destruction of the Mordgris, to finding out what happened to my mother. Ilene should *want* that, she should *thank* me for it even.

Even if the Mordgris don't steal the map away, what if the crew votes against it? What if they choose La Isla de Oro instead?

My hand hovers over the drawer, shaking, and then…my decision is made. And I can't turn back from it. I won't.

I swipe the map from the drawer, tuck everything else back into place, and vanish out of the captain's quarters, into the night.

And like the Mordgris in my bedroom, it's as if the map and I were never there at all.

*From the ship's articles of the* Lady Luck:

*No children shall be kidnapped, pressed into service of the* Luck, *or harmed.*

My hands tremble when I shut the door to my quarters firmly behind me. The map, tucked inside my shirt for safekeeping, is a brand against my skin.

What did I do? What did I *just* do?

I sit down hard on my bunk, fighting the equally strong instincts to leave the map safe against my skin or take it out and turn it over, examining it carefully.

I can't *really* have done this. I'd raised such hell against Captain Ilene for taking a choice from the crew, and here I am, securing the map from them, violating every rule that we stand for. We're a *family*, damn it. You don't steal from family.

But it's my *mother*.

My resolve firms. It's not really stealing if I give the

map back when I'm done with it. It's not as though I'm trying to rouse a mutiny on-board, after all. I only need it for a little while. But I can't do it entirely alone.

I think, first, of Sam. But she's crew, just like me. Were it any other situation, I know exactly what I'd do if one of the other crew members came to me with property filched from the captain's chambers. I'd secure the stolen bounty, kindly escort the betrayer to the brig, and report the theft. I'd be sorry about it, if it were Sam. But, I'd rationalize, she'd have known the risks.

No. I can't tell Sam. I can't tell *anyone* on the *Luck's* crew.

That's why I find myself standing over Leo—the real Leo—sleeping in the small bunk he and John have been allotted. The Wesson brothers are curled together, two small safe harbors for each other.

If I wasn't shaking, the magnitude of what I've done continuing to wash over me like the aftershock of a quake, I might have had time to stop and admire that sort of complete trust in another person.

But only in a dreamworld do I have that time. Instead, I shake Leo awake, fighting the wave of nausea that washes over me at the touch, remembering the Mordgris who wore his face stroking my skin.

Leo comes to immediately, bolting upright. I jump backward, trying to put some distance between us as he puts a protective arm over John's body, an instinctive reaction to a moment where his body perceives danger. Their hammock swings with the movement. John mumbles and turns over in his sleep.

Leo squints into the darkness, relaxing when his eyes adjust to the lack of light. "Grace?" His voice is muddled with sleep, thick with dreams that still cling to him. He's forgotten that he's supposed to be mad at me.

Wordlessly, I hold out the map, and he straightens. "*Grace.*" He says my name again, tone incredulous this time. "What are you doing? What have you *done?*"

He casts a glance back at John, who is still sound asleep. Then he makes a noise that's somewhere between a grunt and a sigh and casts his covers aside, seizing me by the arm and marching me into the corner of the room. The vast chamber belowdecks where their hammock hangs is hardly private. Several other members of the crew have their sleeping quarters in here, and everywhere we are surrounded by the deep breathing, the snores, the unconscious sighs of their slumber.

"I don't know much about piracy," he says, flicking eyes that are at once worried and angry down from the map and up to me. "But I am relatively certain that stealing your crew's prized bounty is *frowned upon.*"

I ignore him. "It's bad. It is, but..."

"Grace, I made a bargain with your captain. And what's more, I am not going to help you get yourself thrown off the ship. I don't care what you say, I am not going to help you translate that."

"I don't need you to translate a gods-damned *word*," I burst out, voice louder than I intended.

He hushes me, eyes wide in alarm, making little shushing motions with his hands, and I bite my lip as someone snores loudly in her sleep.

"I don't need you to translate the map for me," I continue on quietly. "I speak the Word of the Ancient Ones. That's not why I'm here."

He reels back. "You speak—then why I am I here, on this ship?" He steps closer. "Why are *you* here now?"

"In case we needed something else from you. And as for me, I—" The words rise in my throat, then fall away because the truth is... "I don't really know," I say honestly.

He's quiet, the only sound between us his contemplative breathing. Even if I can't see him, I can feel him, his gaze raking over my face, searching for answers he won't find. "Why do you want the map, Grace?"

I reach for a dismissive laugh, but even to my ears, it sounds forced. "Why else? Treasure, of course."

A pause. And then, in a soft voice, vacant of pretense, he asks, "Why do you *really* want it?"

And, in the face of a question uttered with such raw, honest curiosity, what else can I do but tell him the truth?

"I want to find my mother."

He blinks. Whatever he was expecting, it wasn't that. "You said..." His brow furrows, and he steps back, eyes flicking around in concentration, trying to remember what I said during our conversation about my mother. "You said that your mother was taken—"

"Taken from me, yes." I'm impatient, waiting for him to get to the point. I know that he'd taken my mother for dead. It's what *everyone* seems to believe, and it was the implication that I'd wanted him to have, that I'd intentionally led him to.

He meets my gaze. "So then...who, exactly, took her?"

And then I tell him. I tell him about the Mordgris, about watching Mama be dragged below the waves. How, in the end, I hadn't been able to tell her from the Mordgris with all of them surrounding her, wearing her face, some of them going so far as to mock the terror on her face, her desperate screams.

I tell him about the Mordgris treasure, about Captain Ilene's choice of La Isla de Oro. And that I'm afraid, when it all comes down to a vote, that I won't win. The Mordgris treasure is a powerful prize, but a dangerous one when you have to fight off a horde of soul- and body-consuming creatures like them. If I didn't have the motivations that I did, the choice for La Isla de Oro would be the obvious one. And one that I fear the crew will choose.

As my explanation lengthens, Leo's body relaxes. His shoulders go from stiff to leaning in toward me, as if pulled into my story. His eyes—so hard, so angry, when he'd stepped out of his hammock—have grown soft. It's almost as if he's longing to comfort me.

My mind flashes to the too-recent experience of the Mordgris in my bed. I'd been so willing to accept Leo's comfort before, when I thought the Mordgris had been him. But now...I can't bring myself to do that.

I meet his eyes and steel myself. "Are you going to help me or not?"

He searches my gaze, looking lost, and shrugs. "Of course I am."

"Good." I swallow hard. "Good, then come with me."

Back and forth, forth and back, I go tonight. From the deck to my quarters, the captain's rooms to mine, and the crew's bunks before I'm back again. Leo's left John tucked safely into their hammock, and we make haste back to my quarters where I have a small lantern that we can work by. I spread the Map of Omna across the floor, smoothing its edges down with care.

As the light of the flame wicks across its parchment,

black lines seep onto the page, curling and spiraling across the blank sheet to fill its surface until nearly every inch is covered in spirals that would do a conch proud. The words of the ancient ones etch themselves into the blank spaces in a bold script, joining seamlessly with the decorative coils. It takes me a moment to adjust before my mind translates it.

*Those who seek shall seeking find*

I swallow hard, heart pounding, then find my tongue, wrapping it around the Word of the Ancient Ones. "Show me the Isle of the Mordgris."

Nothing happens.

That...isn't possible. I flick my gaze up to Leo and try again. "I need to find the Mordgris," I say in a harsher tone.

Nothing.

Lost, I look to Leo, who, though his expression remains largely disapproving, lets his lip quirk up into a reluctant smirk. He leans low over the map, fingers splayed wide over its edges, and whispers, in the lovely, lilting accent:

*"Seekers seek what you may find."*

It's like the words were a key, turning a lock. The text and spirals vanish, as though sucked back inside the map.

I look up at Leo, brow furrowed in confusion.

Now, he grins. "Come now," he says. "You didn't think I'd give you *all* of my secrets, did you? I had to keep *something* back so you all found me useful."

That's the precise reason we *did* keep him on-board. Still, I'd have thought he could share that the map needed a bloody *password*.

I suppose he wasn't quite as arrogant as he seemed. He'd never thought his position guaranteed and tucked this small nugget away in his back pocket for safekeeping.

"I suppose I'd have done the same," I grumble. My gaze moves back to the blank parchment, which remains empty. "Is it...broken?" I look up at Leo as though he has the answer.

And apparently, my trust in him here has merit. He *does* have this answer. When his eyes meet mine, they're warm, encouraging. Though a least a yard separates us, it's as supportive as if he's laid his hands on my shoulders for me to lean back against him.

Just as I'd leaned against the Mordgris who wore his form like a cloak.

I banish that thought. It's not the time. And if I succeed with this map, none of the Mordgris will be able to pull such a trick ever again.

"Ask again," he urges me.

When I speak now, my voice is barely above a whisper. "Show me..."

It's on the tip of my tongue to ask the map to show me my mother, but I don't think that I could stand the disappointment if it were to go blank again. That flash of hope, once a small spark, has only recently become a steady flame. This belief that somehow, some way, she survived— I'm not ready for the possibility that it could be snuffed out so soon.

"Show me where the Mordgris come from," I say.

There is a pause. A moment, where the map remains blank. A heartbeat in which my hopes linger on the edge of a cliff, poised to plummet on the rocks below. And then, as if it is reacting to a cue that both Leo and I are deaf to, the map springs into action.

Ink races across its surface, sketching a sea of lines, waves drawn black and turbulent. An invisible pen draws a ship—ours, the *Luck*— straight down to the details of our flag flying high above it. The map is alive with movement. Our sails and flag flutter in the map's wind. The ship undulates along the inky waves.

Next, is a compass etched in the corner, then a series of dashed lines from the ship, across the sea, marking a route plagued with creatures, rocky outcroppings, and shapes in the sea that I don't recognize; islands given names that I've never heard.

There is another pause, where it seems for a minute as if the map has shown us a route to nowhere. And then— almost as if it is reluctant, for it is drawn far slower than its previous renderings—the unmistakable form of a Mordgris appears. Clawed hands. Black eyes and blank face. Needle teeth.

I shudder.

Behind that, in fits and starts, an island appears behind it. And on the island's far north corner, finally, a wary, hesitant X.

It's far. A journey, no doubt about that. Past any islands I recognize and not a stretch of land that I could flit off to while the others are occupied on Cavellia or another spot we're more likely to frequent. No, this is a place that has to be planned for.

But I'm an experienced sailor. I know how to determine a heading. I'm more than capable of translating shapes on a map to what I see in front of me.

What's stopping *me* from making those plans?

Shaking, I snatch the map up. This is it. A clear route to the Mordgris. This is exactly what I hoped for. My eyes race over the parchment, and I scarcely even notice the obstacles drawn between the island and the *Luck*.

And *sod* Captain Ilene. She doesn't want to go after my mother or the Mordgris? *Fine.* But *I* have the map now and I'll—

Like a bucket of cold water is tossed over my head, I freeze. I'll what? I have no ship with which to make this mission if it's voted against. No crew.

I have to leave the *Luck*.

My mind goes numb with clarity. I put the map back

down and carefully roll it back up.

A hand on my wrist stops me. "Grace. What are you doing?"

I snatch my hand free and continue to roll the parchment. "The crew will never vote to go after the Mordgris. I'll have to go alone."

"You will *not.*"

My eyes dart up to his, my heart longing to just agree to take him along. It would be so *nice* to have a companion on this mad quest. But…

"You hate fighting, Leo. I don't expect to get through this without some bloodshed."

He shrugs and grins sheepishly. "You'll teach me to be better. Or we'll get me a pistol. I'm not overly choosy. You take your pick."

Very still, almost afraid to move, I search his eyes for any flickers of doubt. "I thought you morally objected to this pirate life of mine."

His hand covers mine once more, fingers squeezing. "They took your mother, Grace. I believe justice is reason enough to join you on this crusade."

My hand turns, palm up, fingers hesitantly lacing with his, at a loss for words. His eyes are soft as they look into mine. And he's so sure, so *confident* that this is the right thing to do to that it's calming. It's the sort of support he and his brother have given each other on-board the *Luck.*

Protection. Companionship.

Gods above. His *brother.*

Reluctantly, I withdraw my hand from the comfort he's provided.

"What of John?"

He hesitates for a moment, but the pause isn't long and drawn out, which tells me that he's already considered this. "I've read your ship's articles. There is a strict ordinance against harming children. And the crew is fond of him. They'll care for him in my stead. He'll be all right."

I take Leo's chin in my hand and make him look into my eyes because I need him to understand how serious I am when I say this. "Chances are that you're right. But, Leo, there was an equally strict rule forbidding that we bring any males on-board. And you and John have been with us for a stretch of time now. They'll be angry when they discover us missing and the map gone. Could you really live with yourself if they decide to take that out on John?"

When he reels back, blinking hard, looking as if I've slapped him, I smile sadly. The idea that John could be punished for his brother's mistakes hadn't occurred to him. I step away.

"It's okay," I say softly. "I can go alone. I'd prefer it, even. You don't need to feel bad about wanting to stay with your brother."

Leo straightens, eyes hardening. "No. John is close to a

man now. I don't want to leave him, but he could come with us."

"Leo, this will be dangerous."

"It's pirates or Mordgris, Grace." He shrugs and smiles, but it fails to reach his eyes. "There is no right choice."

I sputter, out of objections. The truth is, if for nothing more than the company, I'd be glad to have him. It would be nice to have someone to watch my back, someone to bounce ideas off of. And Leo has already proved to have intimate knowledge of the map. I could not have unlocked it alone. What if I run into more challenges with it? Then, I'd be alone. Ship-less, crew-less, and with a map to nowhere.

I sigh and return his shrug, half-smiling. "If you think it's the right choice...I'd be glad to have you along."

This time, the smile lights a few dim sparks in his eyes. "I need to wake John," he says. "I'll meet you by the longboats?"

I nod. "Be quick about it. This will be difficult enough with the night watch. Once the day's light is upon us..."

I don't need to complete my sentence. He nods and is out of the room in the space of a breath. I grab the pack I usually take onto land expeditions and hurriedly begin to shove supplies into it. A compass. A bedroll. A canteen. Another canteen.

I swear. We won't make it three days without food and

water to fill these canteens. I peer out the porthole and gauge the position of the moon in the sky. Daylight isn't far off, but night lingers long enough that I think I have time to make the necessary trip to the kitchens and steal some badly needed rations before climbing aboard a longboat, hoisting its sail with the Wessons, and casting off into the unknown.

I cast a last glance back at the room that's been my home since being elected quartermaster. There's nothing left in here for me now. All that matters is finding the Mordgris.

And hopefully, Mama along with them.

The mess is quiet when I slip through it, pack on my back, and into the galley, searching for food. I disregard biscuits and hardtack immediately. They'll be useless the instant water hits them. But apples...those won't last for long. They're on the verge of turning already, but I'll take them. They're less likely to be missed if someone comes looking for an early morning bite.

The last thing we need is the whole crew looking to find us on the horizon before we've even set sail. The *Luck* could easily catch us if they know to look out for us. But not if they don't know where to look. If they think that we're still in our quarters, sleeping... if they don't immediately take the map out for examination... they might not realize that we're missing right away. It could buy us a few hours before they're in pursuit.

Maybe, maybe, maybe. This expedition has barely begun, and already it's chock full of unknown variables.

Once I fill the remainder of my pack and canteens, I slip between the darkness of the barrels and galley counters and head for the stairs, the promise of the longboats beyond them.

But I don't make it out of the galley. My way is blocked by a figure standing on the last few steps.

"Ah, Gracie." Captain Ilene steps into the light of the moon leaking in among the hanging pots, dancing among the dust motes. Her hair is mussed. Her clothes are rumpled. She'd dressed in a hurry.

When she speaks again, her voice sounds torn between a sob and a sigh. "I had hoped it wouldn't be you."

*From the ship's articles of the* Lady Luck:

*She who commits theft against the* Luck *shall be marooned and left with a pistol. It will be loaded with a single shot.*

# 12

"Captain..." I start, eyes darting around for some sort of excuse. The only ones that I find are ones that I know she'll see through immediately. But without any other options, I use one of those excuses anyway. "I was just...looking for an evening snack." I ease my pack to the floor to free my hands, moving cautiously and keeping my hands where she can see them.

She snorts and takes another step down the stairs, boots clunking. "I think you can do better than that."

"No...I really can't."

The clothes she must have hurriedly thrown on aren't her nightclothes; she's not dressed for bed. She's dressed for *battle*. Her pistol is holstered, her sword in its scabbard at her hip. I can't see them, but I'd bet gold that a dagger is tucked into her right boot, and her hat is tilted back so that her field of vision is clear.

I am not dressed for bed either. My hand hovers over the hilt of my sword.

Ilene's eyes track my every movement, her gaze flitting down to my hand, at the ready above my weapon. The smile she gives me is tinged with sadness. "Is this how it's going to be, Gracie?"

I draw, the metal singing its morose but resolute tune as its drawn from its sheath. "I think this is how it has to be, Captain."

Her smile vanishes. Her eyes become hard, calculating. "So be it, then."

In a single, fluid movement, Ilene draws her weapon and lunges toward me, but I am ready for her. My sword bolts up to meet hers, steel clanging as they crash against each other.

I grit my teeth and shove back with all of my might. I won't lose so quickly. I won't give up the battle before it's begun.

She staggers backward and looks up at me with newly assessing eyes. Ilene and I have dueled many times before. Always, *always*, I have wanted to win. And always, *always*, she has bested me. But this time is different and I think we both sense that. There are stakes this time, and I mean to win. I'm fighting for more than just my pride. More, even, than for my hopes of finding my mother, of revenge.

The penalty for stealing from the *Lady Luck* and her crew is marooning on a desert island. It might as well be a death sentence. I'm fighting for my *life*.

It's with that thought ringing through my head that I match Ilene strike for desperate strike.

My defenses seem weak in the face of her frenzied attack. I can barely keep up with the maelstrom she unleashes upon me. I'd never realized before how she much she held back in our practice duels. She didn't want to hurt me before. That's changed now.

My blocks are beginning to flag, my blade getting up to fend her off in the nick of time. I need to change tactics and quickly. I can already feel my arms straining with the effort of meeting the captain's assault. And defending against an onslaught like Ilene's, I'll run out of energy fast. If I want to get past her and meet Leo at the longboats, I'll need to do more than just defend myself. I need to go on the attack.

But *how*, when matching her is all I've managed so far?

"Admit it," I pant, desperate for a distraction. "You never intended to go after the Mordgris, whether I succeeded with the crew's vote or not." The need for conversation is feigned, but the bitterness in my voice doesn't need to be. The muscles in my arms ache in tandem with my heart as I press her back.

"Fine," she spits. Ilene's fingers grip the hilt of her sword as she applies still more pressure upon mine. The veins on the backs of her hands are stark with the strain as a bead of sweat snakes its way over her forehead. "I admit to it freely."

It brings me no joy to hear it, but my strength is renewed by the bolt of anger that shoots through me. Simple swordplay will no longer do, I think, and I cry out as I kick at her legs. Not expecting the retaliation from that avenue, she starts back, and I succeed in throwing her off me.

Now, I'm on the offense, sword flying toward her as fast as the words spill from my mouth, accusations hurtling through the air as quickly as my attacks. "How can you say that so easily? So *casually*? Does treasure matter so much to you that you can't even bring yourself to entertain the *idea* of revenge on the Mordgris? You never even wanted to go after my *mother*." My voice breaks on the word.

And though my weapon still hasn't struck her, she winces as that attack strikes true.

"Of *course* I wanted to go after her." Ilene's cry is a broken one, full of frustration. Her eyes remain on my sword, tears beading at their corners, but they're unfocused now, seeing me, but no longer truly *seeing* me. She's somewhere else entirely.

And I feel absolutely no qualms about using that to my advantage. I bear down on her, sword singing as I parry, parry, then, seizing my first real opening, thrust.

The captain's sword clatters as it's flung across the floor. She falls to her knees before me.

For the first time, I am the victor between us.

"Of course I wanted to go after your mother, Grace," Ilene repeats quietly. She keeps her gaze directed downward, flinching as I press in toward her. She's right to be worried. Not even I know what I plan to do. I can barely see beyond the haze of my anger, but I stop before her, the point of my sword trembling in the air between us.

She continues to speak, voice low, her fist clenched at her side. "I *desperately* wanted to go after her. But she made me promise that I wouldn't."

A drop of water dots the floor below. Ilene's sweat or tears? And if they're tears...are they real or feigned? I wouldn't put it past her to put on a show in order to think of a way out of my grasp.

Suddenly, my sword feels even heavier.

"*Liar,*" I accuse. My voice shakes with uncertainty. "Why would she do that?"

Ilene's voice takes on the lilt of a storyteller. Though she's the one telling me this fairy story, her tone is somehow far away. "I always assumed she thought your father would come for her. For years, it was like we were actors doomed to put on the same play every night. Our little romance. Daily, we'd dutifully repeat the same lines. We'd go to bed. I'd tell her I loved her. She'd swear the same. And then, she'd wring the same promise from me, night after night.

"'If I am ever taken,' she'd say, eyes dark and intense as she looked up at me. 'I want you to take Grace and sail away. Do not come after me.'

"And every night, I would laugh it off. 'Don't *worry*. No man or woman will take you from me, my love,' I'd say. I'd brush a curl behind her ear, with a reassuring kiss dropped lightly onto her lips."

Her lips twist in a bitter smile. "In the end, I was right. No man or woman took her. Instead, it was creatures that I could never hope to best. And what could I do but keep my promise? How could I lose you both?"

Ilene bows her head even lower when she's finished.

Do I believe her?

I feel like I can't breathe. My breath is ragged, tearing into the silence between us as though it has teeth to rend it in two.

Finally, Ilene can't take the pressure anymore. I can *feel* her need to look up at me and gauge what I am thinking. It's a palpable force in the air.

She lifts her eyes to mine and gasps. "Grace. Your eyes..."

My blade nudges her throat, daring her to say more. "What about them?"

Her gaze moves away, unable to hold my stare, locking on the weapon at her neck. She swallows. "They're...*black*."

Now I am certain that she is only keeping up a charade. Oh, she's an actor, all right. Just like she said. But her play is different this time.

It's not a romance, but a tragedy. My eyes fixate on the veins in her neck; blue, but if I spill them upon the floor, it will be a beautiful, glorious red. The color of war. The color *victors* wear when they are painted in their enemy's blood.

I am suddenly, ravenously, deliriously thirsty.

My sword presses to her neck, drawing forth a bead so dark it resembles a drop of ink.

"*Do you take me for a fool?*" I ask in a deadly whisper.

My voice is the only thing that saves Ilene.

It doesn't *sound* right. The words are correct, certainly. But the pitch, the sibilance...all of it comes out wrong. It warbles and twists on every word. Familiar, but not my own.

I sound...like my mother.

The similarity strikes, and I drop my sword, sending it clattering to the ground, but I'm practically deaf to it.

A mirror. I need a mirror. I stagger toward the pots and pans hanging in the galley, the only reflective surfaces within reach. Grabbing one with shaking hands, I force myself to look.

My eyes aren't just black. They're *inky* black.

The soulless black of a Mordgris's eyes.

There's a great clang as the pot crashes to the ground. My hands wind themselves into my hair, desperately trying to soothe myself.

"*What is happening to me?*"

Ilene's voice this time, but it came from my mouth.

"I'd like that answer myself." Metal, cool to the touch, rests upon my throat as Ilene's sword snakes around me. I hadn't even noticed her get up. I raise my hands in surrender.

"I yield."

*From the ship's articles of the* Lady Luck*:*

*A crew member accused of violating the ship's articles has the right to stand before her peers and attempt to muster a defense.*

# 13

S tripped of the map and my weapons, the sun is rising, casting a fiery glow across the sea as I'm marched across the deck at the behest of Ilene's sword. She even took Mama's compass from me.

I am utterly alone.

The late-night revelers have long since passed out or gone to sleep in their bunks, but the morning crew has begun to stir. I keep my head bowed low as the gasps of those already on deck reach my ears.

It must be quite the sight, I think. I try to picture it from their point of view. The captain, leading her loyal quartermaster toward the brig. They must be wondering: *They're as close as a mother and her daughter, so who betrayed who?* Is the captain punishing the quartermaster unjustly or has she done something to earn it? The quartermaster's arms are akimbo. Her palms are on the back of her head. And her eyes...

Can they see my eyes? Are they still black?

The inquiries begin.

"Grace?"

"Captain, what's happened?"

"*Grace.*" One voice is louder than the rest. Sam's hat falls to the deck as she jogs to keep pace with the captain's efficient stride. "Grace, what's going on?" She turns frantically to Captain Ilene. "Captain, what are you *doing?*"

I don't have to turn to know that the captain's jaw is clenched. I can hear it clearly in her reply. "Miss Porter has seen fit to relieve the *Lady Luck* of some her cargo, Miss Smi."

Sam stops, looking relieved. She laughs. The captain keeps walking, and so I do as well. "Is *that* what you think? That she *stole* from the *Luck?* Captain, it's obvious you've just made a mistake. Grace would *never—*"

"You shouldn't defend me, Sam. I would," I interrupt, keeping my eyes forward. The door to the brig below waits ahead of me, wood dark, hinges rusty. "I did."

I chance a glance back at her and manage to catch a glimpse of her face, stark with horror, painted with shock. She hasn't managed to fasten her jaw closed before Captain Ilene and I descend the steps to the brig.

My feet fall heavy on the staircase, their echoes muffled and suppressed by the suffocating environment. The air is dark down here and stale somehow. The salty sea breeze that's so prevalent on deck doesn't reach below to these neglected bowels of the ship. The gravity of my situation presses in on me more and more the lower we go.

The *Luck* doesn't often have occasion to take prisoners, so our brig is small and ill-attended. The iron bars are rusted in places, slick with inexplicable moisture in others. Someone threw dry hay inside one of the holdings in a poorly conceived attempt to either make it more comfortable or to soak up the damp. Either way, they failed.

When we stand before the two small cells, Ilene uses words, not her sword, to prod me forward. "Get in," she says quietly.

I obey, stepping forward to stare blankly at the discolored brown wall. Water slicks down its surface, and I frown, making a mental note to discuss that with Jane. Water shouldn't be able to get in here—

I have to stop that chain of thought. I won't be discussing anything with Jane anymore. Or any of the crew. Concerns of the ship are no longer *my* concern.

"What happens now?" I ask, voice vacant of expression.

"You should know what happens next. You're our quartermaster." Ilene says my title like it tastes sour. "What do the ship's articles say?"

Indeed, I am the quartermaster. And I'd been a good one, too. I can rattle off the ship's articles backward and forward. I know the rules well. I broke them anyway. "Crew shall not steal from crew. She who commits theft against the Luck shall be marooned and left with a pistol." My eyes close. "It will loaded with a single shot," I recite without emotion.

When I turn, opening my eyes, the captain is nodding, face distraught. My eyes catch on the bead of clotted blood at her neck. I study it, remembering how drawn to it I felt, waiting for that thirst, that hunger to strike me again, but it is absent. There's only me, my guilt, and the burning, steadfast knowledge that I would seize the same opportunity that landed me here again and again if given the chance. Even knowing there's only the slimmest possibility of success. Even knowing I'm doomed to failure. I'd have to try.

"Why did you do it, Grace?"

I shrug, helpless, feeling unwelcome tears prick at the corners of my eyes. "There was a chance I could find Mama. How could I not?"

Ilene reaches through the bars to take my face in her hands. Her voice and expression are full of grief, eyes swimming with sorrow. "I don't know if they killed her. I don't know if she lives on. But she is lost to us either way. You must know that the Mordgris will never give her back."

In the face of everything I've done, all that I'm about to lose, I'm not willing to admit that. I can't let the possibility that I've done all of this for *nothing* stand.

If Ilene really believes what she says, how can she fight her way free of the same need for revenge that I feel? I'll never understand it.

"They'll *never* give her back, Grace," she says firmly, giving me a little shake as though trying to press this belief into me.

I remain silent, and she steps away, looking lost.

"They won't," she repeats quietly, and this time, it's almost to herself. "But because of what you've done, now I'll lose you both."

Her footfalls as she climbs the stairs and leaves me are the soft heartbeat of my life on the *Lady Luck*, fading slowly away.

I spend a sleepless day and night belowdecks, listening to the distant sounds on the deck as the news of my treachery sweeps the crew. Try as I might to strain my ears, attempting to catch the specifics of any conversation is pointless. The distance between us is too great. But I don't need to know the precise content of the dialogue to glean the topic. The tone of the words above me carries well. There's an air of shock, an undercurrent of betrayal. There are murmurs of anger, of the need for revenge. I recognize the notes of these emotions instantly. They and I are well-acquainted.

At some point, they wrestle Leo down the stairs. They must have found him dilly-dallying near the longboats, trying to act casual. He's forced into the cell adjacent to mine, and almost instantly, he surges up against the bars, talking quickly, urgently. Hushed plans of overpowering a guard, getting John, sprinting toward the longboats.

I'm not sure if his hopes are brave or stupid.

"Leo," I say dully. "Leave it."

"*Leave* it?" he asks, aghast. "Grace, they'll kill us."

I laugh, taking him by surprise. "No, they won't," I say. And I must sound very confident, for he sags in relief. "We'll be marooned on an island. They won't *need* to do any killing. They'll be happy to let us handle the dirty business of death ourselves."

His mouth firms. "My brother is to be left alone on this ship," he says. "I refuse to die."

I nod. I'd nearly forgotten about young John. Of course Leo would want to fight for him. Same as I would fight to the death for Sam or my mother. "That's fair. It's good to know where we stand when we're on the island, then."

This sets him off again, a torrential downpour of words falling from his lips, but I am deaf to them. I curl up in the corner and await my fate.

It's Anne they send for me the next day, with Bonnie and old Maude behind her to ensure my compliance. I scoff internally, rising to my feet. I suppose I should feel flattered that they feel three people are required to escort me above. As though, stripped of my weapons, I have a hope of overpowering any of them long enough to make a break for one of the longboats.

And even if I could, where would I go? I have no map. No plotted course. Nothing but the clothes on my back to my name.

Anne's expression is unsympathetic as she unlocks the cell door. "Come on, then," she says. "They're all waiting for you."

A crowd of the crew greets me when we get above deck. The sky that greets me is a half-hearted sort of gray, a reluctant wind blowing through my hair as I'm marched toward Captain Ilene—and Celia.

My heart twists. Have the captain and crew really been so quick to replace me? Wearing a smug expression, Celia's standing right where she's always wanted, where *I* used to stand. Ilene's second-in-command.

Sam's face is still the same mask of horror she wore when I was paraded past her to the brig, and when Anne and the others march me by her, I think I hear her whisper, "What have you done?"

The captain's speech enumerating my crimes against the *Luck* is short, but exceedingly effective. The crew is supposed to be my family, but what I'd done had been a very quick betrayal. I'd tried to deprive them of a bountiful prize, of the freedom to vote and make decisions—the power that we'd all sought out in a life upon the sea.

And whether the crew is a family or not, it's still a family of pirates, so when the captain's voice, wavering with emotion, suddenly gives out, Celia takes up the mantle, stirring her audience into a rowdy crowd, all of them hailing her and calling for my head upon a fire. Weapons are thrust into the air. They spit when my name is spoken.

"Our ship's charter is very clear," Celia says, voice strong, in an echo of what I'd thought only hours before. "Any member of the crew who steals from the ship shall be marooned and left with a single bullet. Grace Porter knew this, and it still wasn't enough to stop her from forsaking all of us. Will anyone here deny that to speak in her defense?"

My heart plummets, looking around. Even Sam is avoiding my gaze. Maude won't look at me. Lila stubs the toe of her boot into the ground. Ilene's eyes are sorrowful when they meet mine. All those who I thought may have something to say—who *might* want to save my life—hold their tongues, remaining silent.

The *Lady Luck* has been my whole life, so though I know that the rules are clear, though I know there is no hope that they'll keep me on-board, I also know with a bone-deep certainty that I have to at least try to stay.

"I'll speak in my own defense," I manage to croak out. "What of the map? You need me to translate."

Disturbed murmurs sweep the crowd. I've managed to drive conflict within the hearts of the crew. Emotions war within them. On the one hand, I'd had the nerve to steal the map and betray them all. On the other, the only way they could see to get at the promised treasure was by using me. Are they really willing to give that up just to punish me?

I fold my hands in front of me to hide how badly they're shaking.

Captain Ilene shakes her head sadly. "Oh, Gracie," she says, so softly that I may be the only one who's heard her. She sounds disappointed in me. I can admit that it was a cheap tactic. But with my life on the line, I'm willing to do what it takes, even if it makes me somehow less in the eyes of her and the crew. "That is why we kept the Wessons on-board," she says, raising her voice. "Lord Leonardo Wesson will act as our translator from this point forward."

The crew almost universally slumps in relief, nodding. I slump, too, but for different reasons. Mine is a slump of defeat. I'd forgotten—we'd *all* forgotten Leo, whose presence they had so protested at first. They'd forgotten the reason the vote had kept him on-board. How useful he could be to them.

He, too, is bound in ropes before them, but his crimes are less than mine. No stolen treasure was found on his person. He may yet save himself from being marooned. At least that's something I can take solace in. Leo will survive. I didn't get the both of us killed today. He'll be able to stay with his brother, exactly as he hoped.

I find little John in the crowd, wrapped up in Maude's pillowy arms as she seeks to comfort him. But little John doesn't look quite so little anymore. He's straightened his back, his eyes are determined, and he and his brother lock gazes. I glance between the two of them. It's as though they're having a conversation none of us can hear, communicating across the deck in silence.

John gives Leo a nod, mouths something I can't catch, and Leo returns it, decisive.

"I won't do it." The voice is Leo's, certain and strong. "I won't translate for any of you if you do this. Leave her on-board or leave me on the island with her."

*What?* My heart plummets to the pit of my stomach.

"What are you doing, you idiot?"

"Saving both of our skins," he shoots back and raises his voice to be heard over the roaring of the crowd. "You'll be left without anyone to translate. The map is useless to you without either of us."

Celia's eyes flash in rage, and her fist crashes toward Leo's head. The edge of her tattoo peeks out from below her sleeve, what looks like the edge of a waving tentacle. Leo lands on his hands and knees before her and glares up. Maintaining eye contact with Celia, he turns his head to the side to spit blood on her boot. Her foot lashes out, finding his vulnerable stomach, before Ilene puts a hand on her shoulder, stopping her.

"That's enough, Celia," she says calmly. Whether she is dismayed over this turn of events, having to abandon me or not, she doesn't show it. The most emotion on her face is disappointment. She has made it very clear to Leo what his standing is on the ship: he doesn't have one. "You have an accord, Mr. Wesson," the captain says, smooth a lake on a windless day. He relaxes, closing his eyes and uttering a soft prayer of thanks.

He didn't let her finish.

"I do hope you enjoy the island."

Leo's eyes open, shooting wide in shock and alarm. "But—"

"It may take some *time*, Mr. Wesson," she interrupts his objections. "But you and Miss Porter are *not* the only ones who speak the Word of the Ancient Ones. I trust we will find another capable translator in your stead."

My heart sinks to my knees as John gives up his attempt at maturity. His wail keens high above the din of the crew. I can't blame him. In his quest to be chivalrous and noble, Leo's lost his brother—and likely his life.

I meet Leo's eyes, and the question I have for him is the same one Sam asked me.

"What have you done?" I whisper. "What have you done?"

*From the ship's articles of the* Lady Luck*:*

*She who attempts a mutiny will have her throat slit and be tossed overboard for the sea to feed upon.*

L eo and I are returned to our cells in the brig. I slump
against the wall, head in my hands, turning over
possibilities in my mind. I've been on islands before.
I'll recognize some of the fruits. We may be able to survive
there for a decent amount of time.

But always there is going to be the lingering presence
of the gun there between us, loaded with a bullet for each
of us.

Somehow, I doubt it will come to that. Now that I've
seen how easily they can leave the water, I suspect the
Mordgris will come for me before long.

Unless they simply drive me to end things first.

Leo paces in his cell, looking worried. "What do you
think is going on up there? Will John be all right?"

I lift my head and sigh, ticking through the possibilities in my mind. We haven't had to maroon anyone since I've been quartermaster, but there was a woman when I was about eleven years old. She'd attempted to conceal a chest full of coins and then smuggle it ashore to sell and keep the profits for herself. Of course, Ilene had caught her and the proceedings had gone forward.

I swallow, and my voice sounds rusty when I speak. "Well, they'll have picked an island and plotted their course by now. They'll want something relatively remote. Nothing in friendly waters where we could spy another island or a mainland that's actually familiar to me.

"When we get there, Ilene will ask for volunteers to row us ashore. They'll retrieve us. Anyone who wants to say goodbye to us will be waiting at the longboats. We'll be given a few moments with them, and then we'll get to the island."

Leo exhales a shaky breath. "And then, we simply...live there? Forever?"

I look straight into his eyes. "We live there. Until we don't. They'll leave us with a pistol. There will be a bullet for each of us in it."

He nods, looking grim. His gaze stares past me, somehow, straight through to what he imagines life on the island will be like. "Should we decide an end is preferable."

"Yes."

He returns to me, to life on-board the *Luck*. "What of John? What will they be doing with him?"

"Nothing at all, if they keep to the charter." I manage a wan smile. "John will be along for a bit of a ride. I suggest you tell him to use the gulls to send missives to any family members or friends that may take him in. If their course finds him somewhere where he may find sympathetic housing, the crew won't hold him captive. He'll be free to go. And until then...he's still very young. They won't force him into battle when they have occasion to clash with other ships."

Some of the tension leaves his shoulders. "He's safe, then?"

My head returns to my palms. "As safe as any of us can be."

It's days before I hear the tell-tale sound of the anchor's chain slowly unwinding, dropping the anchor to bury itself in shallow waters. Leo, curled up into himself on the floor, jerks awake, looking around in alarm for the source of the sound. His eyes snag on me. "What's happening?"

"This is it," I say. "They've found an island."

Leo and I will have to fend for ourselves from here on out if we want to survive. Until now, they've continued to provide us with small rations of food and water, albeit much smaller ones than we'd enjoyed while working on-board. Ilene won't let us starve while we're still on her ship. She'll let the island do that work for her. Lila had been one of our servers, then Katya another day.

Lila had spit on the food before she handed it through the bars, sneering. "What a waste of perfectly good food," she'd said, "when those of us who don't dip into the crew's pockets could be eating it."

She'd left, and not one to waste otherwise good food, I'd eaten immediately. Leo, face twisted in revulsion, had held out for hours until his hunger got the best of him.

I rise to my feet, and Leo hastily follows to do the same, brushing hay and dirt from his knees. There's hardly a point. Neither of us has bathed in days. We're still in the same clothes we'd worn when we'd tried to make a break for it with the map. My eyes linger on the stairs to the brig, waiting to see who our volunteers are.

The light hits Celia first as she enters the brig. One corner of her mouth is tugged up into a smirk. Behind her, without much of a surprise, are Anne and Bonnie. The one friendly face that emerges is Maude's. Kindly, old Maude, whose galley I'd run through as a child. I'm glad that hers will be one of the last faces that I see.

Celia gives me a warning look as she dangles the key before the lock. "Don't try anything," she says. "The captain's insistent we remain faithful to the ship's articles and simply give you a marooning, but there's a ship full of women who wouldn't cry over your blood shed." She unleashes a full-fledged grin, no longer needing to hide her disdain for me beneath a thin veneer of respect. "Me? I think we should have just let the Mordgris have you." Her face presses between the bars and whispers. "After all, they seemed to like your mother well enough."

I surge against the bars, hand reaching through to seize a fist-full of Celia's hair. My other hand goes for her throat as the bars press into her flesh, pillowing around her cheeks. "Say one more thing about my mother," I dare her, before Bonnie and the others manage to free her from my grip.

Celia coughs, massaging her throat and glaring at me. "I think perhaps Mr. Wesson should go first," she manages to say once she's caught her breath.

"All four of you for little me?" Leo asks. "I'm flattered. Truly."

"No," Celia says flatly, failing to respond with any semblance of good humor. "You'll go with Maude. We'll escort Miss Porter above deck." Anne and Bonnie smirk behind her, plenty amused for themselves.

Celia hands Maude the keys, and she unlocks Leo's cell, motioning him out calmly. "Come on, lad. Best be getting on with it."

He stares at her, at a loss for words. I think he'd readied himself for Celia's brand of escorting—this sort of caustic wit and veiled violence. But Maude's gentle resignation is something he isn't prepared for. His mouth opens, then closes, not finding an appropriate response. He sighs, shoulders slumping. "I suppose you're right."

He and Maude climb the stairs side by side, no hands upon him. Maude isn't afraid he'll fight. Isn't afraid that he'll run.

After all, where would he go?

The clanging of the keys against my cell door crashes like a cymbal as Anne whips them to the side, turning the lock. I brace myself. There will be no gentleness for me. Leo was just a man. I am a woman. A member of the crew. One who betrayed all of them. I barely had the respect of Celia and her cohorts before. Now, they take pleasure in my pain. Their fingers dig into the flesh of my upper arms as they seize me, and I wince, marching up the stairs. I'll have bruises with their fingerprints.

I thought the crew would be gathered to see the welcome sight of Leo and I sailing away, but this is somehow worse. The ladies are simply...going about their duties. Katya swabs the deck, glaring at me from the corner of her eye. I look up to the crow's nest. Rae is lounging there, comfortable as can be. A gull flies overhead, a message strapped to its legs as it wings toward its recipient.

Lila leans against one of the larger cannons, sternly lecturing one of the young gunners, and Jane is on her hands and knees, nailing a loose board securely back into place. Neither of them pay me any mind.

The only ones waiting for us at the longboats are Ilene and John. My heart sinks. I thought that, if no one else, there would be at least be Sam. But she's nowhere to be found.

John can barely get a word out through his tears, and Leo has knelt before him, speaking softly. John rubs at his eyes, still sniffling. The last-minute words of wisdom his brother is imparting upon him seem to be having a calming effect upon him.

"Can't I go with you?" his little voice asks, clogged with emotion.

"Shh, shh," Leo hushes him. "No, we can't have that. You've got to carry on the Wesson name. The king will be looking to us as his loyal subjects. We can't let him down."

"But—"

I turn to Ilene while Leo tries to assuage his brother's fears for the future. He can't take away the pain, but at least they can say goodbye. It's more than Mama and I got.

Even if I'd been given the chance, I wouldn't have known *how* to say goodbye to Mama. Just as I don't know how to handle saying it to Ilene. How do I bid a forever farewell to the woman who might as well have been a second mother to me?

I square my shoulders. "Captain," I start stiffly. "It's been—"

I don't get to finish my thought. Ilene lunges toward me, pulling me into her body for a tight hug. My eyes widen in shock, unexpected tears springing to their corners. Hesitantly, my hands come up to her shoulder blades, and when she doesn't withdraw, only grips me to her harder, I bury my face in her neck, letting the tears flow freely.

"I'm sorry," I whisper, voice choked around my stifled sobs.

She pulls me back to look into my eyes, searching for something. The darkness in them? Ilene grips my arms before dropping a fierce kiss upon my cheek and whispering into my ear.

"Don't use the gun, Grace. Whatever you do."

Something drops into my pocket, the weight of it registering against my thigh. My hand reflexively moves to check it, but Ilene catches my eye and shakes her head in warning. "For love and luck," she whispers.

Whatever it is, she doesn't want Celia and the others to know about it. My heart lurches in hope, mind racing. If she doesn't want me to use the pistol, maybe she'd just given me something else. Something that can save me and Leo from our fate on the island.

"Give them the guns," Ilene orders when she steps away.

Celia mouth unfurls into a slow smile. "I think you mean give *her* the gun, Captain."

The captain's brow furrows. "A bullet and a pistol for each of them," Ilene says. "As the ship's articles lay out."

Anne tuts. "A bullet and a pistol for each marooned member of the *crew*," she says. She sneers in Leo's direction. "It doesn't say anything about a marooned *man*."

Bonnie pouts out a lip in feigned sympathy, assuming a babyish falsetto. "Only one of you will get the quick death."

"I suppose you'll just have to decide which one." Celia looks exceedingly satisfied in delivering this news. Voice jovial, she slings an arm around Leo's shoulder that he immediately shrugs off, expression filled with distaste. "Who knows how the other will go? Dehydration, sun poisoning, starvation... The future is positively *rife* with possibilities."

"Here you go then, Miss Porter." Maude is quiet as she uncurls her fingers from around the pistol, as black as my eyes had been and just as scary.

Leo's eyes drift down toward the pistol and then back toward me. I waste no more time in contemplating what may be. I snatch the gun from Maude's grip and tuck it securely into my waistband with shaking hands. Survival is the name of the game for me. There's no question in my mind that if it comes down to me or Leo...it's me.

I'll choose me every time.

"Go on," Captain Ilene says, nodding toward the longboats, where Maude and Bonnie have already climbed in. Ilene has grown strangely calm. The anger she'd held toward me has disappeared. Her sorrow, vanished. Her expression is implacable as Leo and I climb aboard the small vessels.

"*Wait!*"

My head whips toward the source of the cry to see Sam sprinting toward us. My spirits lift a little bit more. She's forgiven me. She came to say goodbye after all.

Sam comes to a screeching halt before the captain and bends over, hands going to her knees as she catches her breath.

"Wait," she pants, holding up a hand.

Celia taps an impatient foot. "We haven't all day, Miss Smi. Say your farewells quickly."

Having regained her composure, Sam straightens, tilting her hat back to reveal her eyes. She meets my gaze. Her irises glitter, and the edge of her mouth is quirked.

Oh no. I know that look.

She's about to do something that I will deeply, *deeply* regret.

"Captain," she announces in a loud voice. "I have stolen from the ship."

A pearl necklace is tossed at Ilene's feet, and she stands open-mouthed in shock as Sam gives her a cheery little salute and climbs aboard the longboat.

"Have you lost your *senses*?" I hiss.

Sam pretends not to hear me.

"*Sam.*"

This time, her eyes slide to me and she rests her hands on mine. "I told you we were family," she says. "You didn't think you were going to get rid of me that easily, did you?"

I am utterly without words as Leo climbs aboard. "Three of us, then?" he checks. "Good. One more brain working to find a way out of this."

"I wouldn't be getting your hopes up, lad," Bonnie says.

The captain recovers from her shock. "Miss Smi, you have the right to stand before your peers and attempt to rally a defense."

"Not necessary, thank you, Captain." She declines the offer with a matter-of-fact tone. "I confessed. I'm to be marooned." Her eyes move to my empty palms. "Have we the pistol?"

Celia starts.

"Give them the second pistol," Ilene orders.

Celia's mouth firms into a displeased little line, but Sam is assuredly another member of the crew, so her arguments based on the ship's articles won't work. We're given another gun, with a second bullet. Much good will that do, but I suppose I should be thankful for any small advantage.

I can't think what Sam hopes to accomplish by doing this. What does any of this change, except that *maybe* the ends of our lives will be a little less lonely? Still, when she squeezes my hand, I squeeze it back. I would have missed Sam.

Finally, Celia climbs aboard the longboat. Anne follows her, clambering on-board and stepping on Leo's foot in what I'm sure is a purposeful mood.

Ilene moves to the railing, watching as Celia and her comrades start to work on the ropes. We slowly lower down the side of the *Lady Luck*. I keep my eyes on Ilene's face, growing smaller and smaller the more the distance between us grows.

Emotion surges within me. "I'll think of you!" I shout on impulse. "All of you."

Ilene pats her pocket, reminding me that she'd put something there. "And I, you, Gracie. Goodbye."

We say no more, but she stays, watching us as the longboat reaches the ocean's surface, taking hold of our small vessel, and I turn my attention from my past to my future.

The island we row toward would look pretty under different circumstances. The sky behind it is clear and blue, the palm trees a verdant green. The white sand looks soft, waves lapping gently at its shore.

It doesn't look like a gravesite. But could be.

As the oars dip rhythmically through the waves, conversation is at a minimum. Both Leo's and Sam's eyes are locked forward on the desert island where we're to spend our foreseeable future. While my former crewmates are focused on depositing us there, I can't take wondering anymore if Ilene gave us a real chance at survival.

My fingers search my pockets, encountering the object Ilene dropped inside.

My spirits sink, instantly recognizing it. After all, I'd held the same object many times over the years.

My mother's compass.

Her *broken* compass. Even if we manage a way off the island, it won't be able to give us a heading. I suppose Ilene had just wanted to provide me with comfort. Not hope. But at least Mama is with me in this small way.

I close my eyes, tilting my face into the sun's warmth until the longboat stutters, bumping into a sandbar. Anne gestures forward. "Off," she says shortly.

Leo, Sam, and I are the first ones off, wading into the water toward the white sandy shores. Already, the sun warms my flesh. I eye the shadows of treeline, pressing Mama's compass into my palm so hard that I'm certain it will leave an indentation. We'll need to get into the shade as soon as possible.

Celia, Anne, and Maude follow, Celia and Anne prodding us forward at swordpoint, while Bonnie waits in the longboat so that it doesn't drift away.

Sand sticks to my sodden clothes as we make it to the island's beach. Salt clings to my mouth. Gods above, I'm already thirsty, and we've barely been here a minute. I take the pistol into my free hand as I run my thumb over the compass, surveying my surroundings

"It's been...interesting, Miss Porter," Celia says in way of a farewell. Her eyes go to my mother's compass, being turned over and over again in my palm, and her eyes shoot wide. "Where did you get—never mind. Hand it over. You're not to have anything but the pistol. Besides, you won't be having much of a use for it anymore."

As her body moves in toward me, her hands angling toward the one thing I have left to call my own, I react on instinct, leveling the pistol against her belly. She freezes instantly.

"I have one shot," I say quietly. "But this belonged to my mother. And I would happily sacrifice a quick and painless death if it meant keeping it from you."

Celia raises her arms in surrender. Her mouth quirks, amused by this last show of defiance. "Fine," she says airily.

"Keep the silly thing. Let it go to waste on your rotting corpse."

She spits into the sand at my feet and twirls a finger for Anne and Maude to follow her back to the ship. Following her example, Anne spits down in the sand as well, but Maude takes a moment to clasp my shoulder.

"I'm sorry it had to end this way, Grace," she says before she, too, wades away.

They clamber into the longboats that will return them to the *Lady Luck* and each take a seat. Except for Celia.

She turns. "Farewell, Miss Porter!" She stands, giving me a mocking wave. And as she does so, her sleeve slides down, finally revealing the tattoo I'd wondered about.

My jaw drops in horror. Even from this distance, it's recognizable: a hissing snake, split into pieces.

It's the broken serpent. Whighorn's symbol.

The pistol falls from numb fingers to nestle in the sand. My heart, already hovering in the pit of my stomach, drops to my toes as the revelation crashes into me.

*That* was who Celia had been sending gulls to. That's why she'd been with him on Cielito. *And* why we had run into him on Cavellia. It hadn't been coincidence. Celia had been informing him all along. Of the map. Of our route. And who knew what else.

Celia follows my gaze, letting out a keening laughing when she sees her tattoo unveiled, bold as you please. "For love and *luck!*' she sing-songs my mother's words, taunting me. I clench an ineffectual fist and rush into the water.

The waves roll into me as I swim determinedly toward the longboats, both Leo and Sam letting out yells of surprise and charging in after me. I barely register their presence. I have to stop Celia before she reaches the *Luck* and makes her betrayal known. I *have* to. I'd taken the map, certainly, but I'd never intended any of them actual harm.

Celia's treachery is the kind with teeth. It will bite.

But my strokes are simply no match for the oars with Anne and Bonnie behind them. Celia drops back down to take her seat, Anne and Bonnie rowing determinedly toward the *Luck*.

I tread water, helpless to do anything but watch them row away. The island, Leo, and Sam are at my back as the longboats draw inexorably closer to the ship. I bob in the tide, this new knowledge hitting me like wave after powerful wave, slamming into me until it threatens to drown me.

There's a snake among the crew of the *Lady Luck.*

And there's absolutely nothing that I can do about it.

*From the ship's articles of the* Lady Luck*:*

*She who attempts a mutiny will have her throat slit and be tossed overboard for the sea to feed upon.*

*Unless, of course, she manages to succeed.*

Grace's story will continue in

# THROUGH FATHOMS
# DARK and DEEP

# Acknowledgments

The Lady Pirates series has been at the fringes of my thoughts for nearly five years now. A scene leapt into my mind and, unable to let it just disappear into the ether, I wrote furiously in order to capture it. But I was neck-deep in writing and revising my debut novel, *Threats of Sky and Sea,* and so, reluctantly, I set it aside to concentrate on the work that I was already doing.

Sometime later, I found myself idly watching Pirates of the Caribbean: The Curse of the Black Pearl and was struck by the fact that Keira Knightley's Elizabeth is the only main female character. (Not altogether surprising, given the landscape of film, but go with me here.)

What if the tables were turned? I thought. What if there was a pirate story revolving around women?

What if there was an entire crew of female pirates?

So, I suppose my first acknowledgments go to the cast and crew of Pirates of the Caribbean, for making me want to even the scales just a little bit.

Next, I want to say a big thank you to my critique partner, Alex Brown. I floundered a lot in writing after concluding my first series, and the encouragement, commiseration, and distraction with other fun projects helped a lot in actually getting this book written.

I also need to thank Lindsey Young, another critique partner. Even from a drastically different timezone, you found the time to read my first few chapters and helped me heave a big sigh of relief when your feedback was largely positive!

Thank you to my editor, Rebecca Gutzmann. My books are always better thanks to your careful eye and thoughtful questions.

The cover of Over Raging Tides was created by Jenny Zemanek of Seedlings Design Studio, and I could not possibly love it more. Jenny, thank you so much for making the perfect cover for my lady pirates.

The interior of this book was formatted by Caitlin Greer and I am very grateful for her incredible work.

I owe a great deal of gratitude to YA Books Central for hosting the cover reveal of Over Raging Tides and to Giselle Cormier of Xpresso Book Tours. I also want to say a preemptive thank you to the reviewers and YA social media influencers who post about and review Over Raging Tides. Half of the battle in publishing is getting a book in front of potential readers, and you all make it a great deal easier.

Thank you to my family, friends, and loved ones who still think it's "cool that I write books." I couldn't do this without your support.

And, of course, if it wasn't for readers like you, I don't know if I would have crawled my way out of the writing hole. Thank you to everyone who has read my work in the past, and thank *you* for reading this book, right now.

Enjoyed this story and wanting more from Jennifer Ellision? You can get the free "Sisters of Wind and Flame" novelette by signing up for her newsletter at https://instafreebie.com/free/0oVts.

# Books by Jennifer Ellision

**Elementals: The Threats of Sky and Sea series:**

Book 1: <u>Threats of Sky and Sea</u>
Book 2: <u>Riot of Storm and Smoke</u>
Book 3: <u>Fall of Thrones and Thorns</u>
<u>Tales from Fire to Frost: A Threats of Sky and Sea collection</u>

**Lady Pirates series:**

Book 1: Over Raging Tides

**New Adult Romance:**

<u>Now and Again</u>

# About the Author

Jennifer Ellision spent a great deal of her childhood staying up past her bedtime with a book and a flashlight. When she couldn't find the stories she wanted to read, she started writing them. She's the author of the young adult fantasy series Elementals: The Threats of Sky and Sea series and the Lady Pirates series. She loves words, has a soft spot for fanfiction, and is a master of what she calls "The Fangirl Flail."

She lives in South Florida with her family, where she lives in fear of temperatures below 60 degrees Fahrenheit. She makes her Internet home at www.jenniferellision.com. You can also find her on Twitter and Instagram @JenEllision. Stay up to date on all of Jennifer's new releases and receive a free novelette by signing up for her newsletter. You can also like her on Facebook as Jennifer Ellision.

Made in the USA
Columbia, SC
13 March 2018